D0923269

KNEEL
TO THE RISING SUN
and other stories

Books by Erskine Caldwell

NOVELS

Journeyman

God's Little Acre

Tobacco Road

SHORT STORIES

We Are the Living

American Earth

Kneel to the Rising Sun

AND OTHER STORIES BY

Erskine Caldwell

New York

THE VIKING PRESS

1935

Some of these stories first appeared in The American Mercury, The Anvil, Direction, Esquire, Literary America, The New Masses, Red Book Magazine, Scribner's Magazine, Story, The Sunday Review, and Vanity Fair.

Printed in U. S. A. by Quinn & Boden Co., Inc., Rahway, N. J.

Distributed in Canada by the Macmillan Company of Canada, Ltd.

for Suzanne

CONTENTS

Candy-Man Beechum

Candy-Man Beechum

IT WAS ten miles out of the Ogeechee swamps, from the saw mill to the top of the ridge, but it was just one big step to Candy-Man. The way he stepped over those Middle Georgia gullies was a sight to see.

"Where you going, Candy-Man?"

"Make way for these flapping feet, boy, because I'm going for to see my gal. She's standing on the tips of her toes waiting for me now."

The rabbits lit out for the hollow logs where those stomping big feet couldn't touch them.

"Don't tread on no white-folks' toes, Candy-Man," Little Bo said. "Because the white-folks is first-come."

Candy-Man Beechum flung a leg over the rail fence just as if it had been a hoe-handle to straddle. He stood for a minute astride the fence, looking at the black boy. It was getting dark in the swamps, and he had ten miles to go.

"Me and white-folks don't mix," Candy-Man told him, "just as long as they leave me be. I skin their mules for them, and I snake their cypress logs, but when the day is done, I'm long gone where the white-folks aint are."

Owls in the trees began to take on life. Those whooping birds were glad to see the setting sun.

The black boy in the mule yard scratched his head and watched the sun go down. If he didn't have all those mules to feed, and if he had had a two-bit piece in his pocket, he'd have liked to tag along with Candy-Man. It was Saturday night, and there'd be a barrelful of catfish frying in town that evening. He wished he had some of that good-smelling cat.

"Before the time aint long," Little Bo said, "I'm going to get me a gal."

"Just be sure she aint Candy-Man's, boy, and I'll give you a helping hand."

He flung the other leg over the split-rail fence and struck out for the high land. Ten miles from the swamps to the top of the ridge, and his trip would be done. The bushes whipped around his legs, where his legs had been. He couldn't be waiting for the back-strike of no swamp-country bushes. Up the log road, and across the bottom land, taking three corn rows at a stride, Candy-Man Beechum was on his way.

There were some colored boys taking their time in the big road. He was up on them before they had time to turn their heads around.

"Make way for these flapping feet, boys," he shouted. "Here I come!"

"Where you going, Candy-Man?"

They had to do a lot of running to keep up with him. They had to hustle to match those legs four feet long. He made their breath come short.

"Somebody asked me where I'm going," Candy-Man said. "I got a yellow gal, and I'm on my way to pay her some attention."

"You'd better toot your horn, Candy-Man, before you open her door. The yellow gals don't like to be taken by surprise."

"Boy, you're tooting the truth, except that you don't know the why-for of what you're saying. Candy-Man's gal always waits for him right at the door."

"Saturday-night bucks sure have to hustle along. They have to strike pay before the Monday-morning whistle starts whipping their ears."

The boys fell behind, stopping to blow and wheeze. There was no keeping up, on a Saturday night, with the seven-foot mule skinner on his way.

The big road was too crooked and curvy for Candy-Man. He struck out across the fields, headed like a plumb-line for a dishful of frying catfish. The lights of the town came up to meet him in the face like a swarm of lightning-bugs. Eight miles to town, and two more to go, and he'd be rapping on that yellow gal's door.

Back in the big road, when the big road straightened

out, Candy-Man swung into town. The old folks riding, and the young ones walking, they all made way for those flapping feet. The mules to the buggies and the sports in the middle of the road all got aside to let him through.

"What's your big hurry, Candy-Man?"

"Take care my dust don't choke you blind, niggers. I'm on my way."

"Where to, Candy-Man?"

"I got a gal what's waiting on her toes. She don't like for to be kept waiting."

"Better slow down and cool those heels, Candy-Man, because you're coming to the white-folks' town. They don't like niggers stepping on their toes."

"When the sun goes down, I'm on my own. I can't be stopping to see what color people be."

The old folks clucked, and the mules began to trot. They didn't like the way that big coon talked.

"How about taking me along, Candy-Man?" the young bucks begged. "I'd like to grab me a chicken off a henhouse roost."

"Where I'm going I'm the cock of the walk. I gouge my spurs in all strange feathers. Stay away, black boy, stay away."

Down the street he went, sticking to the middle of the road. The sidewalks couldn't hold him when he was in a hurry like that. A plateful of frying catfish, and he would be on his way. That yellow gal was waiting, and there was no time to lose. Eight miles covered, and two short ones to go. That saw-mill fireman would have to pull on that Monday-morning whistle like it was the rope to the promised land.

The smell of the fish took him straight to the fish-house door. Maybe they were mullets, but they smelled just as good. There wasn't enough time to order up a special dish of fins.

He had his hand on the restaurant door. When he had his supper, he would be on his way. He could see that yellow gal waiting for him only a couple of miles away.

All those boys were sitting at their meal. The room was full of hungry people just like him. The stove was full of frying fish, and the barrel was only half-way used. There was enough good eating for a hundred hungry men.

He still had his hand on the fish-house door, and his nose was soaking it in. If he could have his way about it, some of these days he was going to buy a barrel of catfish and eat them every one.

"What's your hurry, Candy-Man?"

"No time to waste, white-boss. Just let me be."

The night policeman snapped open the handcuffs, and reached for his arms. Candy-Man stepped away.

"I reckon I'd better lock you up. It'll save a lot of

trouble. I'm getting tired of chasing fighting niggers all over town."

"I never hurt a body in all my life, white-boss. And I sure don't pick fights. You must have the wrong nigger, white-boss. You sure has got me wrong. I'm just passing through for to see my gal."

"I reckon I'll play safe and lock you up till Monday morning just the same. Reach out your hands for these cuffs, nigger."

Candy-Man stepped away. His yellow gal was on his mind. He didn't feel like passing her up for no iron-bar jail. He stepped away.

"I'll shoot you down, nigger. One more step, and I'll blast away."

"White-boss, please just let me be. I won't even stop to get my supper, and I'll shake my legs right out of town. Because I just got to see my gal before the Monday-morning sun comes up."

Candy-Man stepped away. The night policeman threw down the handcuffs and jerked out his gun. He pulled the trigger at Candy-Man, and Candy-Man fell down.

"There wasn't no cause for that, white-boss. I'm just a big black nigger with itching feet. I'd a heap rather be traveling than standing still."

The people came running, but some of them turned around and went the other way. Some stood and looked at Candy-Man while he felt his legs to see if they could hold him up. He still had two miles to go before he could reach the top of the ridge.

The people crowded around, and the night policeman put away his gun. Candy-Man tried to get up so he could be getting on down the road. That yellow gal of his was waiting for him at her door, straining on the tips of her toes.

"White-boss, I sure am sorry you had to go and shoot me down. I never bothered white-folks, and they sure oughtn't bother me. But there aint much use in living if that's the way it's going to be. I reckon I'll just have to blow out the light and fade away. Just reach me a blanket so I can cover my skin and bones."

"Shut up, nigger," the white-boss said. "If you keep on talking, I'll just have to pull out my gun again and hurry you on."

The people drew back, so they would not stand too close. The night policeman put his hand on the butt of his gun, where it would be handy in case.

"If that's the way it's to be, then make way for Candy-Man Beechum, because here I come."

The Walnut Hunt

The Walnut Hunt

WHEN Church came up the street after dinner, he had one of his father's oat sacks that was large enough to hold a barrelful of walnuts. I had got a forty-eight-pound flour sack, and was waiting for him at the corner.

"We'll break our backs carrying these big sacks full of walnuts," I said when Church stopped and showed me his. "Why didn't you get a smaller one?"

"Why didn't you?" Church said.

"It's the only one I could find. We don't have to get them full, anyway. I'd be satisfied with mine half full this time."

"Same here," he said. "Come on. We won't have time to find even a pocketful if we don't hurry. I'll bet somebody's out there in the woods beating us to them right this minute."

We went up to the end of the street and crossed the cotton field behind P. G. Howard's barn bordering the road. The field was about half a mile wide, and beyond the field were the woods where we hunted walnuts every fall. There were lots of walnut trees there, but the woods were so large that sometimes it took a long time to find any.

"I hope we get some whoppers this time, Ray," Church said, running down the cotton rows and jumping over the dried-up stalks. "I'd like to take home enough to fill a washtub, after they're hulled and dried out."

The year before we brought home three or four loads of them, and after they had been hulled and spread out in the sun to ripen, we put away enough to last us almost all winter.

"How about last year?" I said. "If we get that many again, we ought to sell some and make a little money."

"There's no fun in that," Church said, picking up a rock and throwing it ahead of us as far as he could. "I'd rather eat them, any day."

We crossed one of the lateral drain ditches that ran from the lower end of town to the creek. The ditch was dry at that time of year, because it carried water off only during the winter rains. Down on the sandy bottom of the ditch were a lot of rabbit tracks. From the way it looked, rabbits must have learned to use the ditches when they were going somewhere so they could keep out of sight of the dogs that were always prowling around the cotton and oat fields looking for them.

Church stood on the side of the ditch and kicked some dirt down to the bottom.

"I'll bet rabbits have a hard time getting out of there when they fall in," he said. "I'd hate to be a rabbit."

"They have a better time than we do," I said. "And, anyway, they have steps and paths they can use when they want to get out."

Church kicked some more dirt down into the ditch. Like all the drain ditches that had been dug near town, it was about six feet deep and two or three feet wide at the bottom. It was not hard to jump across any of them, but dogs and rabbits fell in sometimes when they were not watching what they were doing.

Church walked backward and got a running start and jumped across, and I followed him. The woods were not far away then, and we did not stop again until we had got there. The oak trees were so tall that they hid all the other trees from sight, and it was hard work looking for walnut trees. After we had gone almost to the other side of the woods, we found a walnut tree, a big one, too; but somebody had beat us to it, and there was not a single one left on the tree or ground. Whoever it was had taken the crop, and they had even hulled some of them there instead of taking them home first.

"That's what I was afraid of," Church said, throwing down his sack and looking at the hulls on the ground. "But I'd like to know who's been getting walnuts in these woods, just the same."

"They couldn't have found them all," I said. "I'll bet there are a hundred more trees all around us."

I started off, and Church picked up his sack and came behind. It was easy to see that he was angry because we had not come sooner. When we got to the other side of the woods, we had not found a single walnut.

"What do you know about that, Ray?" he said, kicking his father's oat sack around on the ground.

"Let's try the grove on the other side of that field," I told him. "There are bound to be walnuts somewhere."

Church picked up his sack and came along, dragging it on the ground behind him.

We had gone half-way across the field towards the second grove when we came to another drain ditch. We were about to jump over it when I happened to see somebody lying on the sandy bottom a dozen yards away. I caught Church by the sleeve before he could jump, and pulled him back.

"What's the matter, Ray?" Church asked.

"Don't talk so loud," I told him, pulling him back out of sight of the ditch. "There's somebody down in there, Church."

"Where?" he said, looking scared.

I pointed where I had seen somebody.

"What are we going to do?" he asked, trembling a little. "We'd better go back home, hadn't we?"

I got down on my hands and knees, and Church dropped beside me, keeping as close as he could.

"Wait till I see who it is," I told him. "I'm going to crawl up there and find out. It's funny for somebody to be out here lying in the bottom of a ditch like that."

Church would not follow me until I had got almost to the edge of the ditch. Then he came hurrying up behind me.

"Don't let anybody see us, Ray," he said. "They might shoot, or something."

I crawled slowly to the side, holding my breath, and looked down at the bottom. Annie Dunn was lying on her back on the sand, staring straight up into the blue sky. Her clothes were knotted around her, and she was covered with streaks of red clay that looked like fresh blood in the sunshine. She was as still as the silence all around us then, but she looked as if she had been having a terrible fight with somebody down there.

Annie lived around the block from us, and she was always going somewhere or coming back. She never stayed at home much after her father got killed in the flour mill, and sometimes her mother came to our house to ask if any of us had seen Annie.

Church caught my sleeve and tried to pull me away. I shook my head and pulled away from him. After a while he stopped trying to make me leave and came back to where I was at the edge of the ditch. Annie had not moved an inch since we first saw her.

"Hello, Annie," I said.

Some pieces of earth broke loose from the side of the ditch and fell tumbling down upon her. She looked straight into our faces.

"What's the matter, Annie?" Church said, so scared he could hardly be still long enough to look at her.

Annie looked straight at us but did not say a word.

"What are you doing down there in the bottom of that ditch, Annie?" I asked her. "You look like you've been fighting somebody down there, Annie."

Annie closed her eyes, and a moment later her face was as white as a boll of cotton. While we watched her, she doubled up into a knot; then she began kicking the sides of the ditch with her feet. One shoe had come off, and the sole of her stocking on her foot was caked with damp red clay. Church backed off a little, but when Annie screamed, he hurried back to see what was the matter with her.

When she had quieted down again, Church looked

at her with his mouth hanging open. "Are you hurt, Annie?" he said. "What's hurting you to make you scream like that? Why won't you say anything, Annie?"

"Why don't you get up from there and go home, Annie?" I asked her.

Annie screamed again, and then she lay still for a while, not making a sound or a motion. Some of the color came back to her face, and she opened her eyes and looked up at us in the same way she had the first time.

"Don't tell anybody, Ray, you and Church," she said weakly. "I don't want anybody to know."

She sounded so much like someone begging you to do something for her that you could not keep from making a silent promise.

"You'd better get up from there, now," Church said.

"I can't," Annie said. "I can't get up, Church."

"Don't you want to?" Church said.

Annie shook her head as much as she could.

"I'm going to tell your mamma, Annie," he said. "If you don't get up from the bottom of that ditch and go home, I'm going straight and tell your mamma."

Annie's face suddenly became white again, and she dug her hands into the sides of the ditch, squeezing the moist red clay until it oozed between her fingers. She began screaming again.

"I'm going home," Church said. "I'm not going to stay here."

I was scared, too, but I did not think we should go away and leave Annie lying there screaming in the bottom of the ditch. I caught Church's sleeve and held him.

Some more dirt broke loose under our hands and fell tumbling down into the ditch upon Annie. She seemed not to notice it at all.

When she stopped screaming and opened her eyes and looked up at us, she did not look like Annie at all. The color had not come back to her cheeks.

"Don't tell anybody, Ray, you and Church," she said weakly. "Will you promise?"

"Why not, Annie?" Church said. "Why don't you want us to tell anybody?"

"I'm having a baby," she said, closing her eyes.

Church leaned so far forward that a whole armful of clay and sand broke loose and fell down into the ditch. Some of it covered one of her legs.

We backed away from the ditch, not getting up from our hands and knees until we were a dozen yards away.

"Let's get away from here," Church said, holding his breath between the words. "I want to go home."

We ran across the field. When we were half-way across, I happened to think about our walnut sacks that we had left at the drain ditch, but I did not say a word to Church about them. When we reached the grove, Church was all out of breath, and we had to stop a minute and lean against some of the trees to get our wind back.

"Do you think Annie's going to die, Ray?" he said, holding his breath between the words and almost choking each time he said one of them.

I did not know what to say. I started running again, and Church began crying because he was behind. By the time we had got to the field behind P.G. Howard's barn, Church was crying so much he could not see where to run. He fell down and tumbled head over heels two or three times, but I did not stop to wait for him to catch up. I kept on running until I got on our front porch.

Horse Thief

Horse Thief

I DIDN'T steal Lud Moseley's calico horse.

People all over have been trying to make me out a thief, but anybody who knows me at all will tell you that I've never been in trouble like this before in all my life. Mr. John Turner will tell you all about me. I've worked for him, off and on, for I don't know exactly how many years. I reckon I've worked for him just about all my life, since I was a boy. Mr. John knows I wouldn't steal a horse. That's why I say I didn't steal Lud Moseley's, like he swore I did. I didn't grow up just to turn out to be a horse thief.

Night before last, Mr. John told me to ride his mare, Betsy. I said I wanted to go off a little way after something, and he told me to go ahead and ride Betsy, like I have been doing every Sunday night for going on two years now. Mr. John told me to take the Texas saddle, but I told him I didn't care about riding saddle. I like to ride with a bridle and reins, and nothing else. That's the best way to ride, anyway. And where I was going I didn't want to have a squeaking saddle under me. I wasn't up to no mischief. It was just a little private business of my own that nobody has got a right to call me down about. I nearly always rode saddle Sunday nights, but night before last was Thursday night, and that's why I didn't have a saddle when I went.

Mr. John Turner will tell you I'm not the kind to go off and get into trouble. Ask Mr. John about me. He has known me all my life, and I've never given him or anybody else trouble.

When I took Betsy out of the stable that night after supper, Mr. John came out to the barnyard and asked me over again if I didn't want to take the Texas saddle. That mare, Betsy, is a little rawboned, but I didn't mind that. I told Mr. John I'd just as lief ride bareback. He said it was all right with him if I wanted to get sawn in two, and for me to go ahead and do like I pleased about it. He was standing right there all the time, rubbing Betsy's mane, and trying to find out where I was going, without coming right out and asking me. But he knew all the time where I was going, because he knows all about me. I reckon he just wanted to have a laugh at me, but he couldn't do that if I didn't let on where I was headed. So he told me it was all right to ride his mare without a saddle if I didn't want to be bothered with one, and I opened the gate and rode off down the road towards Bishop's crossroads.

That was night before last—Thursday night. It was

a little after dark then, but I could see Mr. John standing at the barnyard gate, leaning on it a little, and watching me ride off. I'd been plowing that day, over in the new ground, and I was dog-tired. That's one reason why I didn't gallop off like I always did on Sunday nights. I rode away slow, letting Betsy take her own good time, because I wasn't in such a big hurry, after all. I had about two hours' time to kill, and only a little over three miles to go. That's why I went off like that.

II

Everybody knows I've been going to see Lud Moseley's youngest daughter, Naomi. I was going to see her again that night. But I couldn't show up there till about nine-thirty. Lud Moseley wouldn't let me come to see her but once a week, on Sunday nights, and night before last was Thursday. I'd been there to see her three or four times before on Thursday nights that Lud Moseley didn't know about. Naomi told me to come to see her on Thursday nights. That's why I had been going there when Lud Moseley said I couldn't come to his house but once a week. Naomi told me to come anyway, and she had been coming out to the swing under the trees in the front yard to meet me.

I haven't got a thing in the world against Lud Moseley. Mr. John Turner will tell you I haven't. I don't especially like him, but that's to be expected, and he knows why. Once a week isn't enough to go to see a girl you like a lot, like I do Naomi. And I reckon she likes me a little, or she wouldn't tell me to come to see her on Thursday nights, when Lud Moseley told me not to come. Lud Moseley thinks if I go to see her more than once a week that maybe we'll take it into our heads to go get married without giving him a chance to catch on. That's why he said I couldn't come to his house but once a week, on Sunday nights.

He's fixing to have me sent to the penitentiary for twenty years for stealing his calico horse, Lightfoot. I reckon he knows good and well I didn't steal the horse, but he figures he's got a good chance to put me out of the way till he can get Naomi married to somebody else. That's the way I figure it all out, because everybody in this part of the country who ever heard tell of me knows I'm not a horse thief. Mr. John Turner will tell you that about me. Mr. John knows me better than that. I've worked for him so long he even tried once to make me out as one of the family, but I wouldn't let him do that.

So, night before last, Thursday night, I rode off from home bareback, on Betsy. I killed a little time down at the creek, about a mile down the road from where we live, and when I looked at my watch again, it was nine o'clock sharp. I got on Betsy and rode off towards Lud Moseley's place. Everything was still and quiet around the house and barn. It was just about Lud's bedtime then. I rode right up to the barnyard gate, like I always did on Thursday nights. I could see a light up in Naomi's room, where she slept with her older sister, Mary Lee. We had always figured on Mary Lee's being out with somebody else, or maybe being ready to go to sleep by nine-thirty. When I looked up at their window, I could see Naomi lying across her bed, and Mary Lee was standing beside the bed talking to her about something. That looked bad, because when Mary Lee tried to make Naomi undress and go to bed before she did, it always meant that it would take Naomi another hour or more to get out of the room, because she had to wait for Mary Lee to go to sleep before she could leave. She had to wait for Mary Lee to go to sleep, and then she had to get up and dress in the dark before she could come down to the front yard and meet me in the swing under the trees.

III

I sat there on Betsy for ten or fifteen minutes, waiting to see how Naomi was going to come out with her sister. I reckon if we had let Mary Lee in on the secret she would have behaved all right about it, but on some account or other Naomi couldn't make up her mind to run the risk of it. There was a mighty chance that she would have misbehaved about it and gone straight and told Lud Moseley, and we didn't want to run that risk.

After a while I saw Naomi get up and start to undress. I knew right away that that meant waiting another hour or longer for her to be able to come and meet me. The moon was starting to rise, and it was getting to be as bright as day out there in the barnyard. I'd been in the habit of opening the gate and turning Betsy loose in the yard, but I was scared to do it night before last. If Lud Moseley should get up for a drink of water or something, and happen to look out toward the barn and see a horse standing there, he would either think it was one of his and come out and lock it in the stalls, or else he would catch on it was me out there. Anyway, as soon as he saw Betsy, he would have known it wasn't his mare, and there would have been the mischief to pay right there and then. So I opened the barn door and led Betsy inside and put her in the first empty stall I could find in the dark. I was scared to strike a light, because I didn't know but what Lud Moseley would be looking out the window just at that time and see the flare of the match. I put Betsy in the stall, closed the door, and came back outside to wait for Naomi to find a chance to come out and meet me in the swing in the yard.

It was about twelve-thirty or one o'clock when I got ready to leave for home. The moon had been clouded, and it was darker than everything in the barn. I couldn't see my hand in front of me, it was that dark. I was scared to strike a light that time, too, and I felt my way in and opened the stall door and stepped inside to lead Betsy out. I couldn't see a thing, and when I found her neck, I thought she must have slipped her bridle like she was always doing when she had to stand too long to suit her. I was afraid to try to ride her home without a lead of some kind, because I was scared she might shy in the barnyard and start tearing around out there and wake up Lud Moseley. I felt around on the ground for the bridle, but I couldn't find it anywhere. Then I went back to the stall door and felt on it, thinking I might have taken it off myself when I was all excited at the start, and there was a halter hanging up. I slipped it over her head and led her out. It was still so dark I couldn't see a thing, and I had to feel my way outside and through the barnyard gate. When I got to the road, I threw a leg over her, and started for home without wasting any more time around Lud Moseley's place. I thought she trotted a little funny, because she had a swaying swing that made me slide from side to side, and I didn't have a saddle pommel to hold on to. I was all wrought up about getting away from there without getting caught up with, and I didn't think a thing about it. But I got home all right and slipped the halter off and put her in her stall. It was around one or two o'clock in the morning then.

The next morning after breakfast, when I was getting ready to catch the mules and gear them up to start plowing in the new ground again, Lud Moseley and three or four other men, including the sheriff, came riding lickety-split up the road from town and hitched at the rack. Mr. John came out and slapped the sheriff on the back and told him a funny story. They carried on like that for nearly half an hour, and then the sheriff asked Mr. John where I was. Mr. John told him I was getting ready to go off to the new ground, where we had planted a crop of corn that spring, and then the sheriff said he had a warrant for me. Mr. John asked him what for, a joke or something? And the sheriff told him it was for stealing Lud Moseley's calico horse, Lightfoot. Mr. John laughed at him, because he still thought it just a joke, but the sheriff pulled out the paper and showed it to him. Mr. John still wouldn't believe it, and he told them there was a mix-up somewhere, because, he told them, I wouldn't steal a horse. Mr. John knows I'm not a horse thief. I've never been in any kind of trouble before in all my life.

They brought me to town right away and put me

in the cellroom at the sheriff's jail. I knew I hadn't stole Lud Moseley's horse, and I wasn't scared a bit about it. But right after they brought me to town, they all rode back and the sheriff looked in the barn and found Lud Moseley's calico horse, Lightfoot, in Betsy's stall. Mr. John said things were all mixed up, because he knew I didn't steal the horse, and he knew I wouldn't do it. But the horse was there, the calico one, Lightfoot, and his halter was hanging on the stall door. After that they went back to Lud Moseley's and measured my foot tracks in the barnyard, and then they found Betsy's bridle. Lud Moseley said I had rode Mr. John's mare over there, turned her loose, and put the bridle on his Lightfoot and rode him off. They never did say how come the halter to get to Mr. John's stable, then. Lud Moseley's stall door was not locked, and it wasn't broken down. It looks now like I forgot to shut it tight when I put Betsy in, because she got out someway and came home of her own accord sometime that night.

Lud Moseley says he's going to send me away for twenty years where I won't have a chance to worry him over his youngest daughter, Naomi. He wants her to marry a widowed farmer over beyond Bishop's crossroads who runs twenty plows and who's got a big white house with fifteen rooms in it. Mr. John Turner says he'll hire the best lawyer in town to take up my case, but it don't look like it will do much good, because my footprints are all over Lud Moseley's barnyard, and his Lightfoot was in Mr. John's stable.

I reckon I could worm out of it someway, if I made up my mind to do it. But I don't like to do things like that. It would put Naomi in a bad way, because if I said I was there seeing her, and had put Betsy in the stall to keep her quiet, and took Lightfoot out by mistake in the dark when I got ready to leave—well, it would just look bad, that's all. She would have to say she was in the habit of slipping out of the house to see me after everybody had gone to sleep, on Thursday nights, and it would just look bad all around. She might take it into her head some day that she'd rather marry somebody else than me, and by that time she'd have a bad name for having been mixed up with me—and slipping out of the house to meet me after bedtime.

Naomi knows I'm no horse thief. She knows how it all happened—that I rode Lud Moseley's calico horse, Lightfoot, off by mistake in the dark, and left the stall door unfastened, and Betsy got out and came home of her own accord.

Lud Moseley has been telling people all around the courthouse as how he is going to send me away for twenty years so he can get Naomi married to that widowed farmer who runs twenty plows. Lud Moseley is right proud of it, it looks like to me, because he's got me cornered in a trap, and maybe he will get me sent away sure enough before Naomi gets a chance to tell what she knows is true.

But, somehow, I don't know if she'll say it if she does get the chance. Everybody knows I'm nothing but a hired man at Mr. John Turner's, and I've been thinking that maybe Naomi might not come right out and tell what she knows, after all.

I'd come right out and explain to the sheriff how the mix-up happened, but I sort of hate to mention Naomi's name in the mess. If it had been a Sunday night, instead of night before last, a Thursday, I could —well, it would just sound too bad, that's all.

If Naomi comes to town and tells what she knows, I won't say a word to stop her, because that'll mean she's willing to say it and marry me.

But if she stays at home, and lets Lud Moseley and that widowed farmer send me away for twenty years, I'll just have to go, that's all.

I always told Naomi I'd do anything in the world for her, and I reckon this will be the time when I've got to prove whether I'm a man of my word or not.

The Man Who Looked like Himself

The Man Who Looked like Himself

EVERYTHING that Luther Branch touched was wont to crumble in his hands like so much desiccated clay. It had always been like that. He was barely able to keep himself alive, and his clothes were always in rags. But no man could truthfully say that Luther had not tried and was not still trying to make a decent living. He worked harder, day in and day out, than any other man in town.

Several years before, one of his efforts to get ahead had been selling fire insurance to storekeepers and house-owners. He failed in that just as he did in everything else he tried to do. It looked as though it were impossible for him to make a dollar.

Once, while he was trying his best to sell insurance, somebody came right out and told Luther that he was not suited to that line of work.

"Luther," the man said, "I can't buy fire protection from you. You don't look like an insurance man."

There was nothing Luther could say, because he knew he did not look like the other men who sold insurance. And, for that matter, he knew he did not look like anyone else in town.

"That's the whole trouble, Luther. You don't look like an insurance man ought to look."

"What do I look like, then?" Luther asked.

"I'll be jumped if I know, Luther. If I could see you in the right job, I'd know for sure; but to save my life I can't figure you out. I suppose you just look like yourself."

Luther Branch did look like himself. Everybody had been saying that since he was a boy, and now that he was past forty, that was all there was to it.

He went into Ben Howard's grocery store early one morning to have a word with Ben. He had been going in there for the past ten or fifteen years to see if Ben had anything to tell him. Ben told him that he ought to start out that same hour and try every kind of known way there was to make money, and to jump from one to the other just as fast as he discovered that he was not suited to a particular line of work.

"It's the only way I know to tell you how to do," Ben said. "I've known you all my life, and we live on the same street, and go to the same church every Sunday, and I want to do everything possible to help you. I've always tried to be your friend. That's why I say the best thing to do is to try everything there is until you find the work you were cut out for. If I could think of a better scheme, I'd certainly tell you about it the minute I heard about it."

"I guess I'll try selling fruit from door to door," Luther said. "It might just as well be that as anything else. It's one line I haven't tried yet. I'll sell fruit."

He went home and got out a push-cart from under the shed and bought it full of oranges and tangerines and grapefruit. He started out trying to sell fruit.

At the first house he stopped he hesitated for a moment at the door before ringing the bell. He had suddenly had a feeling that fruit-selling was not his life-work, either. He started to turn around and go back home without even making an effort to sell anything. He would take the fruit back to the store where he had got it on credit and turn it all back.

"Good morning, Mr. Branch," somebody said.

He was half-way down the steps when he heard the woman speaking to him. He stopped and looked around at her standing in the doorway.

"What have you for sale today, Mr. Branch?" she asked pleasantly.

"Fruit, Mrs. Todd," he answered.

"What kind of fruit? Citrous?"

Luther knew by the tone of Mrs. Todd's voice that she was in the market for citrous fruit. He felt better then, because he was certain he would be able to make a sale. He ran out to the street and brought back several baskets and set them down in front of her on the porch. He stepped back, taking off his hat, and waited for her to select the fruit she wished to buy.

"The oranges are nice-looking," Mrs. Todd said, rolling one in her hand. "And I've been looking for some large juicy grapefruit. How much are they, Mr. Branch?"

"The grapefruit are . . ."

She looked up at Luther then, waiting for him to quote prices to her. Their eyes met for a second, and Luther choked on something in his throat. He coughed and rubbed his neck, but he could not force a single word from his lips after that. Mrs. Todd had averted her eyes, but she looked up into his face again. He knew at that moment that it was hopeless. It had always been like that. It did not matter whether it was insurance, fruit, soap, china doorknobs, or second-hand automobiles that he was attempting to sell. When people stopped and looked at him, the deal was off. He had never yet looked like the thing he was trying to sell.

There was a long period of silence when nothing was said. Mrs. Todd stepped back towards the door, glancing at Luther. Luther picked up the baskets and backed down the steps in the direction of the push-cart in the street. By the time he had reached it, the woman had gone into the house and had closed the door behind her.

On the way home with the empty cart, after having returned the unsold fruit to the store, Luther felt as if there was not any use in his trying to make a living any longer. The best thing for him to do, he told himself, was to apply for admittance to the county poor farm. That was all that was left for him to do. He was ready to quit trying after almost a lifetime of effort to make a living.

The next day he stopped at Ben Howard's store for a moment. Ben was busy at the time, but he motioned to Luther to wait until he was free. Luther waited until the customer had left the store, and Ben came up to him in front of the candy counter.

"How did you make out selling oranges and grapefruit yesterday, Luther?"

Luther shook his head, allowing it to fall forward until his eyes were staring at the oiled floor at Ben's feet.

He was getting ready to tell Ben that he had decided to go to the county poor farm when Ben slapped him heavily on the shoulder, causing him to forget what he had in mind to say.

"Now, Luther, you might think it was none of my business again, but I'm your friend and I want to help. This is what I've got to say, Luther. I've thought of something else for you to try. Go get yourself a—"

Somebody burst through the door, throwing it wide

open, and ran up to the counter where Ben and Luther were standing.

"What's the trouble, Henry?" Ben asked as soon as he could see who it was. "You ran in here like something was after you behind. What's the matter?"

"I've got to find somebody quick to butcher a hog for me, Ben. One of my five-hundred-pounders broke out of the barn and got run over in the street by a truck just a few minutes ago. I've got to find somebody to butcher it for me right away. The weather's too hot for me to waste any time over it. Who can I get to help me?"

"Why don't you get Jim Hall, down at the market, to do it for you, Henry?" Ben said. "That's his trade."

"I just now spoke to Jim, but he's all alone in the market today, and he can't close up. I've got to find somebody else. I've got to have a man in a hurry. He needn't be a finished butcher, because I can help do some of the work myself. But I need somebody to pitch in right away!"

Luther started for the door, leaving them both silent while they searched their minds for a butcher. Just as he got to the door, Ben caught up with him.

"Looks like you ought to know somebody in town, Luther, who could help Henry with his hog."

Henry came forward and stared Luther in the face. His mouth hung open for several moments while he stared. Ben, too, had begun to stare at Luther by that time. Luther looked from one to the other bewilderedly. He thought they were going to accuse him of having run down the fattening hog and killed it.

"Well, I'll be a son of a gun!" Henry said, stepping back to survey Luther from head to toe. "I'll be a son of a gun if I won't!"

Luther stood at the door, not knowing what to do. He waited for one of them to say what it was that had caused them both to stare at him so hard.

Presently, Henry glanced at Ben and walked up to Luther, putting his hand on his shoulder.

"You're the man, Luther. I'll be a son of a gun if you aren't."

"He's right, Luther," Ben said. "Henry's dead right. You're the man."

Luther started to protest.

"I didn't run over a hog in the street, Ben. I don't even own a truck. And you know good and well I couldn't even kill a chicken with that little push-cart of mine."

"No! No! Luther," Henry protested. "I didn't try to accuse you of killing my hog. You're all mixed up. You're the man I'm looking for to butcher it for me. Why, Luther, you even look like a butcher!"

Both men had become excited.

"All your troubles are over now, Luther," Ben said.

"You won't have to worry again for the rest of your life. You'll own your own market before the year is out, and everybody in town will be buying their meat from you. It's going to be hard on Jim Hall, but there's no help for that. Maybe, after you get started, you can hire Jim to help you. But don't let him stay up front. It's your place to stay up front in full view where the people can see you."

Henry was nodding his head emphatically.

"When people buy something, Luther," Henry said, "they want the man who's selling it to look like the thing they're buying. It hasn't failed to be true since the world began."

"But I haven't any money to start a meat market," Luther protested.

"You let me take care of that part," Ben said. "You don't have to worry about anything any more. You just stay like you are."

Luther shoved his hands deep into his pockets where his gripped fingers would be safe from sight. He was even trembling a little.

"Why didn't you tell me that before, Ben?" he asked shakily. "Here I am, past forty years old, and I've been a failure all my life. If I had known about that twenty years ago, I wouldn't be in the fix I'm in now. Why didn't you say it sooner?"

"I didn't know it myself, Luther, till just now when

Henry started talking about a butcher. I suppose it needed just something like what Henry said to bring it out. But there's no mistaking it now, Luther. I know what I see when I see it."

Henry went to the door.

"Let's hurry, Luther. We've got to get that hog quartered before night."

Luther went out on the sidewalk in front of the store and stopped to look across the street towards Jim Hall's meat market. His head went up erectly, his shoulders went back, and his thick, heavy body stiffened. He was still looking at the market when Henry caught him by the sleeve and pulled him up the street.

As they turned the corner, Luther looked back over his shoulder once more, and then he started walking briskly up the street with Henry at his side. He was walking so fast by that time that Henry was finding it difficult to keep up with him.

Maud Island

Maud Island

UNCLE MARVIN was worried. He got up from the log and walked towards the river.

"I don't like the looks of it, boys," he said, taking off his hat and wiping his forehead.

The houseboat was drifting downstream at about three miles an hour, and a man in a straw hat and sleeveless undershirt was trying to pole it inshore. The man was wearing cotton pants that had faded from dark brown to light tan, and the perspiration from his body was turning them back to their first color.

"It looks bad," Uncle Marvin said, turning to Jim and me. "I don't like the looks of it one whit."

"Maybe they are lost, Uncle Marvin," Jim said. "Maybe they'll just stop to find out where they are, and then go on away again."

"I don't believe it, son," he said, shaking his head and wiping the perspiration from his face. "It looks downright bad to me. That kind of a houseboat never has been out for no good since I can remember."

On a short clothesline that stretched along the starboard side, six or seven pieces of underclothing, the kind that women wear, hung waving in the breeze.

"It looks awful bad, son," he said again, looking down at me.

We walked down towards the river and waited to see what the houseboat was going to do. Uncle Marvin took out his plug and cut off a chew of tobacco with his jackknife. The boat was swinging inshore, and the man with the pole was trying to beach it before the current cut in and carried them back to midchannel. There was a power-launch lying on its side near the stern, and on the launch was a towline that had been used for upstream going.

When the houseboat was two or three lengths from the shore, Uncle Marvin shouted at the man poling it.

"What's your name, and what do you want here?" he said gruffly, trying to scare the man away from the island.

Instead of answering, the man tossed a rope to us. Jim picked it up and started pulling, but Uncle Marvin told him to drop it. Jim dropped it, and the middle of the rope sank into the yellow water.

"What did you throw my rope in for?" the man on the houseboat shouted. "What's the matter with you?"

Uncle Marvin spat some tobacco juice and glared right back at him. The houseboat was ready to run on the beach.

"My name's Graham," the man said. "What's yours?"

"None of your business," Uncle Marvin said. "Get that raft away from here."

The houseboat began to beach. Graham dropped the pole on the deck and ran and jumped on the mud flat. He called to somebody inside while he was pulling the rope out of the water.

The stern swung around in the backwash of the current, and Jim grabbed my arm and pointed at the dim lettering on the boat. It said *Mary Jane*, and under that was *St. Louis*.

While we stood watching the man pull in the rope, two girls came out on the deck and looked at us. They were very young. Neither of them looked to be over eighteen or nineteen. When they saw Uncle Marvin, they waved at him and began picking up the boxes and bundles to carry off.

"You can't land that shantyboat on this island," Uncle Marvin said threateningly. "It won't do you no good to unload that stuff, because you'll only have to carry it all back again. No shantyboat's going to tie up on this island."

One of the girls leaned over the rail and looked at Uncle Marvin.

"Do you own this island, Captain?" she asked him.

Uncle Marvin was no river captain. He did not

even look like one. He was the kind of man you could see plowing cotton on the steep hillsides beyond Reelfoot Lake. Uncle Marvin glanced at Jim and me for a moment, kicking at a gnarled root on the ground, and looked at the girl again.

"No," he said, pretending to be angry with her. "I don't own it, and I wouldn't claim ownership of anything on the Mississippi, this side of the bluffs."

The other girl came to the rail and leaned over, smiling at Uncle Marvin.

"Hiding out, Captain?" she asked.

Uncle Marvin acted as though he would have had something to say to her if Jim and I had not been there to overhear him. He shook his head at the girl.

Graham began carrying off the boxes and bundles. Both Jim and I wished to help him so we would have a chance to go on board the houseboat, but we knew Uncle Marvin would never let us do that. The boat had been beached on the mud flat, and Graham had tied it up, knotting the rope around a young cypress tree.

When he had finished, he came over to us and held out his hand to Uncle Marvin. Uncle Marvin looked at Graham's hand, but he would not shake with him.

"My name's Harry Graham," he said. "I'm from

up the river at Caruthersville. What's your name?"

"Hutchins," Uncle Marvin said, looking him straight in the eyes, "and I aint hiding out."

The two girls, the dark one and the light one, were carrying their stuff across the island to the other side where the slough was. The island was only two or three hundred feet wide, but it was nearly half a mile long. It had been a sandbar to begin with, but it was already crowded with trees and bushes. The Mississippi was on the western side, and on the eastern side there was a slough that looked bottomless. The bluffs of the Tennessee shore were only half a mile in that direction.

"We're just on a little trip over the week-end," Graham said. "The girls thought they would like to come down the river and camp out on an island for a couple of days."

"Which one is your wife?" Uncle Marvin asked him.

Graham looked at Uncle Marvin a little surprised for a minute. After that he laughed a little, and began kicking the ground with the toe of his shoe.

"I didn't quite catch what you said," he told Uncle Marvin.

"I said, which one is your wife?"

"Well, to tell the truth, neither of them. They're just good friends of mine, and we thought it would be a nice trip down the river and back for a couple of days. That's how it is."

"They're old enough to get married," Uncle Marvin told him, nodding at the girls.

"Maybe so," Graham said. "Come on over and I'll introduce you to them. They're Evansville girls, both of them. I used to work in Indiana, and I met them up there. That's where I got this houseboat. I already had the launch."

Uncle Marvin looked at the lettering on the *Mary Jane*, spelling out *St. Louis* to himself.

"Just a little fun for the week-end," Graham said. "The girls like the river."

Uncle Marvin looked at Jim and me, jerking his head to one side and trying to tell us to go away. We walked down to the edge of the water where the *Mary Jane* was tied up, but we could still hear what they were saying. After a while, Uncle Marvin shook hands with Graham and started along up the shore towards our skiff.

"Come on, son, you and Milt," he said. "It's time to look at that taut line again."

We caught up with Uncle Marvin, and all of us got into the skiff, and Jim and I set the oarlocks. Uncle Marvin turned around so he could watch the people behind us on the island. Graham was carrying the heavy boxes to a clearing, and the two girls were unrolling the bundles and spreading them on the ground to air.

Jim and I rowed to the mouth of the creek and pulled alongside the taut line. Uncle Marvin got out his box of bait and began lifting the hooks and taking off catfish. Every time he found a hook with a catch, he took the cat off, spat over his left shoulder, and dropped it into the bucket and put on new bait.

There was not much of a catch on the line that morning. After we had rowed across, almost to the current in the middle of the creek mouth, where the outward end of the line had been fastened to a cypress in the water, Uncle Marvin threw the rest of the bait overboard and told us to turn around and row back to Maud Island.

Uncle Marvin was a preacher. Sometimes he preached in the schoolhouse near home, and sometimes he preached in a dwelling. He had never been ordained, and he had never studied for the ministry, and he was not a member of any church. However, he believed in preaching, and he never let his lack of training stop him from delivering a sermon whenever a likely chance offered itself. Back home on the mainland, people called him Preacher Marvin, not so much for the fact that he was a preacher, but because he looked like one. That was one reason why he had begun preaching at the start. People had got into the habit of calling him Preacher Marvin, and before he was forty he had taken up the ministry as a calling. He had never been much of a farmer, anyway—a lot of people said that.

Our camp on Maud Island was the only one on the river for ten or fifteen miles. The island was only half a mile from shore, where we lived in Tennessee, and Uncle Marvin brought us out to spend the week-end five or six times during the summer. When we went back and forth between the mainland and the island, we had to make a wide circle, nearly two miles out of the way, in order to keep clear of the slough. The slough was a mass of yellow mud, rotting trees, and whatever drift happened to get caught in it. It was impossible to get through it, either on foot or in a flat-bottomed boat, and we kept away from it as far as possible. Sometimes mules and cows started out in it from the mainland to reach the island, but they never got very far before they dropped out of sight. The slough sucked them down and closed over them like quicksand.

Maud Island was a fine place to camp, though. It was the highest ground along the river for ten or fifteen miles, and there was hardly any danger of its being flooded when the high water covered everything else within sight. When the river rose to forty feet, however, the island, like everything else in all directions, was covered with water from the Tennessee bluffs to the Missouri highlands, seven or eight miles apart.

When we got back from baiting the taut line, Uncle Marvin told us to build a good fire while he was cleaning the catch of catfish and cutting them up for frying. Jim went off after an armful of limbs while I was blowing the coals in the campfire. Jim brought the wood and built the fire, and I watched the pail of water hanging over it until Uncle Marvin was ready to make the coffee.

In the middle of the afternoon Uncle Marvin woke up from his midday nap and said it was too hot to sleep any longer. We sat around for ten or fifteen minutes, nobody saying much, and after a while Uncle Marvin got up and said he thought he would walk over to the other camp and see how the people from Caruthersville, or Evansville, or wherever they came from, were getting along.

Jim and I were up and ready to go along, but he shook his head and told us to stay there. We could not help feeling that there was something unusual about that, because Uncle Marvin had always taken us with him no matter where he went when we were camping on the island. When Jim said something about going along, Uncle Marvin got excited and told us to do as he said, or we would find ourselves being sorry.

"You boys stay here and take it easy," he said. "I've got to find out what kind of people they are before we start in to mix with them. They're from up the river, and there's no telling what they're like till I get to know them. You boys just stay here and take it easy till I get back."

After he had gone, we got up and picked our way through the dry underbrush towards the other camp. Jim kept urging me to hurry so we would not miss seeing anything, but I was afraid we would make so much noise Uncle Marvin would hear us and run back and catch us looking.

"Uncle Marvin didn't tell them he's a preacher," Jim said. "Those girls think he's a river captain, and I'll bet he wants them to keep on thinking so."

"He doesn't look like a river captain. He looks like a preacher. Those girls were just saying that for fun."

"The dark one acted like she's foolish about Uncle Marvin," Jim said. "I could tell."

"That's Jean," I said.

"How do you know what their names are?"

"Didn't you hear Graham talking to them when they were carrying their stuff off that houseboat?"

"Maybe he did," Jim said.

"He called that one Jean, and the light one Marge."

Jim bent down and looked through the bushes.

"Uncle Marvin's not mad at them now for coming here to camp," he said.

"How can you tell he's not?" I asked Jim.

"I can tell by the way he's acting up now."

"He told Graham to get the houseboat away from here, didn't he?"

"Sure he did then," Jim whispered, "but that was before those two girls came outside and leaned over the railing and talked to him. After he saw them a while he didn't try to stop Graham from landing, did he?"

We had crawled as close as we dared go, and fifty feet away we could see everything that was going on in Graham's camp. When Uncle Marvin walked up, Graham was sitting against the trunk of a cypress trying to untangle a fishing line, and the two girls were lying in hammocks that had been hung up between trees. We could not see either of them very well then, because the sides of the hammocks hid them, but the sun was shining down into the clearing and it was easy to see them when they moved or raised their arms.

Five or six cases of drinks were stacked up against one of the trees where the hammocks were, and several bottles had already been opened and tossed aside empty. Graham had a bottle of beer beside him on the ground, and every once in a while he stopped tussling with the tangled fishing line and grabbed the bottle and took several swallows from it. The dark girl, Jean, had a bottle in her hand, half full, and Marge was juggling an empty bottle in the air over her head. Everybody looked as if he was having the best time of his life.

None of them saw Uncle Marvin when he got to the clearing. Graham was busy fooling with the tangled fishing line, and Uncle Marvin stopped and looked at all three of them for almost a minute before he was noticed.

"I'll bet Uncle Marvin takes a bottle," Jim said. "What do you bet?"

"Preachers don't drink beer, do they?"

"Uncle Marvin will, I'll bet anything," Jim said. "You know Uncle Marvin."

Just then Graham raised his head from the line and saw Uncle Marvin standing not ten feet away. Graham jumped up and said something to Uncle Marvin. It was funny to watch them, because Uncle Marvin was not looking at Graham at all. His head was turned in the other direction all the time, and he was looking where the girls lay stretched out in the hammocks.

He could not take his eyes off them long enough to glance at Graham. Graham kept on saying something, but Uncle Marvin acted as though he was on the other side of the river beyond earshot.

Jean and Marge pulled the sides of the hammocks over them, but they could not make Uncle Marvin stop looking at them. He started to grin, but he turned red in the face instead.

Graham picked up a bottle and offered it to Uncle Marvin. He took it without even looking at it once, and held it out in front of him as if he did not know he had it in his hand. When Graham saw that he was not making any effort to open it, he took it and put the cap between his teeth and popped it off as easily as he could have done it with a bottle-opener.

The beer began to foam then, and Uncle Marvin shoved the neck of the bottle into his mouth and turned it upside down. The foam that had run out on his hand before he could get the bottle into his mouth was dripping down his shirt-front and making a dark streak on the blue cloth.

Jean leaned out of her hammock and reached to the ground for another bottle. She popped off the cap with a bottle-opener and lay down again.

"Did you see that, Milt?" Jim whispered, squeezing my arm. He whistled a little between his teeth.

"I saw a lot!" I said.

"I didn't know girls ever did like that where everybody could see them," he said.

"They're from up the river," I told him. "Graham said they were from Evansville."

"That don't make any difference," Jim said, shaking his head. "They're girls, aren't they? Well, whoever saw girls lie in hammocks naked like that? I know I never did before!"

"I sure never saw any like those before, either," I told him.

Uncle Marvin had gone to the tree at the foot of one of the hammocks, and he was standing there, leaning against it a little, with the empty bottle in his hand, and looking straight at them.

Graham was trying to talk to him, but Uncle Marvin would not pay attention to what Graham was trying to say. Jean had turned loose her sides of the hammocks, and Marge, too, and they were laughing and trying to make Uncle Marvin say something. Uncle Marvin's mouth was hanging open, but his face was not red any more.

"Why doesn't he tell them he's a preacher?" I asked Jim, nudging him with my elbow.

"Maybe he will after a while," Jim said, standing on his toes and trying to see better through the undergrowth.

"It looks to me like he's not going to tell them," I

said. "It wouldn't make any difference, anyway, because Uncle Marvin isn't a real preacher. He only preaches when he feels like doing it."

"That doesn't make any difference," Jim said.

"Why doesn't it?"

"It just doesn't, that's why."

"But he calls himself a preacher, just the same."

"He doesn't have to be a preacher now if he doesn't want to be one. If he told them he was a preacher, they'd all jump up and run and hide from him. They think he's a man just like Graham is."

Uncle Marvin was still standing against the tree looking at the dark girl, and Graham was a little to one side of him, looking as if he didn't know what to do next.

Presently Uncle Marvin jerked himself erect and turned his head in all directions listening for sounds. He looked towards us, but he could not see us. Jim got down on his hands and knees to be out of sight, and I got behind him.

The three others were laughing and talking, but not Uncle Marvin. He looked at them a while longer, and then he reached down to the top case against the cypress and lifted out another bottle. Graham reached to open it for him, but Uncle Marvin bit his teeth over the cap and popped it off. The beer began to foam right away, but before much of it could run out, Uncle Marvin had turned it up and was drinking it down.

When the bottle was empty, he wiped his mouth with the back of his hand and took three or four steps towards the dark girl in the hammock. Jean kicked her feet into the air and pulled the sides of the hammock around her. The other girl sat up to watch Uncle Marvin.

All at once he stopped and looked towards our camp on the other side of the island. There was not a sound anywhere, except the sucking sound in the slough that went on all the time, and the sharp slap of water against the sides of the houseboat. He listened for another moment, cocking his head like a dog getting ready to jump a rabbit, and broke into a run, headed for our camp. Jim and I just barely got there before Uncle Marvin. We were both puffing and blowing after running so fast, but Uncle Marvin was blowing even harder and he did not notice how short our breath was. He stopped and looked down at the dead fire for a while before he spoke to us.

"Get ready to go home, son, you and Jim," he said. "We've got to leave right now."

He started throwing our stuff into a pile and stamping out the ashes at the same time. He turned around and spat some tobacco juice on the live coals and grabbed up an armful of stuff. He did not wait for us to help him, but started for our skiff on the mud flat right away with a big load of stuff in both arms. Jim and I had to hurry to catch up with him so he would not forget and leave us behind.

He took the oars from us and shoved off without waiting for us to do it for him. When we were out of the mouth of the creek, he took his hat off and threw it on the bottom of the skiff and bent over the oars harder than ever. Jim and I could not do a thing to help, because there were only two oars and he would not turn either one of them loose.

Nobody said a thing while we were rowing around the slough. When we got within a hundred feet of shore, Uncle Marvin started throwing our stuff into a heap in the stern. We had no more than dragged bottom on shore when he picked up the whole lot and threw the stuff on the dried mud. The pans and buckets rolled in every direction.

Both of us were scared to say a word to Uncle Marvin because he had never acted like that before. We stood still and watched him while he shoved off into the river and turned the skiff around and headed around the slough. We were scared to death for a while, because we had never seen anybody cut across so close to the slough. He knew where he was all the time, but he did not seem to care how many chances he took of being sucked down into the slough. The last we saw of him was when he went out of sight around Maud Island.

We picked up our things and started running with them towards home. All the way there we were in too much of a hurry to say anything to each other. It was about a mile and a half home, and upgrade every step of the way, but we ran the whole distance, carrying our heavy stuff on our backs.

When we reached the front gate, Aunt Sophie ran out on the porch to meet us. She had seen us running up the road from the river, and she was surprised to see us back home so soon. When we left with Uncle Marvin early that morning, we thought we were going to stay a week on Maud Island. Aunt Sophie looked down the road to see if she could see anything of Uncle Marvin.

Jim dropped his load of stuff and sank down on the porch steps panting and blowing.

"Where's your Uncle Marvin, Milton?" Aunt Sophie asked us, standing above me and looking down at us with her hands on her hips. "Where's Marvin Hutchins?"

I shook my head the first thing, because I did not know what to say.

"Where's your Uncle Marvin, James?" she asked Jim.

Jim looked at me, and then down again at the steps.

He tried to keep Aunt Sophie's eyes from looking straight into his.

Aunt Sophie came between us and shook Jim by the shoulder. She shook him until his hair tumbled over his face, and his teeth rattled until they sounded as if they were loose in his mouth.

"Where is your Uncle Marvin, Milton?" she demanded, coming to me and shaking me worse than she had Jim. "Answer me this minute, Milton!"

When I saw how close she was to me, I jumped up and ran out into the yard out of her reach. I knew how hard she could shake when she wanted to. It was lots worse than getting a whipping with a peach-tree switch.

"Has that good-for-nothing scamp gone and taken up with a shantyboat wench again?" she said, running back and forth between Jim and me.

I had never heard Aunt Sophie talk like that before, and I was so scared I could not make myself say a word. I had never heard her call Uncle Marvin anything like that before, either. As a rule she never paid much attention to him.

Jim sat up and looked at Aunt Sophie. I could see that he was getting ready to say something about the way she talked about Uncle Marvin. Jim was always taking up for him whenever Aunt Sophie started in on him.

Jim opened his mouth to say something, but the words never came out.

"One of you is going to answer me!" Aunt Sophie said. "I'll give you one more chance to talk, Milton."

"He didn't say where he was going or what he was going to do, Aunt Sophie. Honest, he didn't!"

"Milton Hutchins!" she said, stamping her foot.

"Honest, Aunt Sophie!" I said. "Maybe he went off somewhere to preach."

"Preach, my foot!" she cried, jamming her hands on her hips. "Preach! If that good-for-nothing scalawag preached half as many sermons as he makes out like he does, he'd have the whole country saved for God long before now! Preach! Huh! Preach, my foot! That's his excuse for going off from home whenever he gets the notion to cut-up-jack, but he never fools me. And I can make a mighty good guess where he is this very minute, too. He's gone chasing off after some shantyboat wench! Preach, my foot!"

Jim looked at me, and I looked at Jim. To save our life we could not see how Aunt Sophie had found out about the two girls from Evansville on Maud Island.

Aunt Sophie jammed her hands on her hips a little harder and motioned to us with her head. We followed her into the house.

"We're going to have a housecleaning around this place," she said. "James, you bring the brooms. Milton, you go start a fire under the wash-pot in the back yard and heat it full of water. When you get it going good, come in here and sweep down the cobwebs off the ceilings."

Aunt Sophie went from room to room, slamming doors behind her. She began ripping curtains down from the windows and pulling the rugs from the floor. A little later we could hear the swish of her broom, and presently a dense cloud of dust began blowing through the windows.

The Shooting

The Shooting

SOMEBODY fired a pistol two or three times, and the reports shook dust loose from the canned goods on the grocery shelves and woke up some of the flies in the display windows.

There had not been so much excitement in town since the morning the bloodhounds tracked the post-office robbers to the vestry of the Methodist church.

The sound of the pistol shots was still ringing in people's ears when two or three dozen men and boys burst out of the stores and made a bee-line for the center of the square, where they could see what was going on. When they got there, most of them were in such a hurry to see something happen that they began running around in circles trying to find it.

"I'd swear that was a .45 that went off," somebody said. "But I don't know a single soul in town who owns anything better than a .38."

Just then a man ran out of the building between the bank and the barbershop, and some of the boys followed him through the square until he stopped, with his back against the brick wall, in front of the drug store. The building he had run out of was a walk-up hotel with a lot of dead flies in the front windows.

Either somebody had telephoned him, or else he had heard the shooting all the way at home, because it was not more than three or four minutes before Toy Shaw, the marshal, came running down the street with his suspenders hanging loose.

"It's still prety early in the day for anybody to be practicing with a gun, or even playing with it," somebody said. "I know I never got up after breakfast to do anything like that."

By that time the housewives who had been downtown doing early shopping were slipping out the back doors of the grocery stores and trying to get home before any more shooting took place. A lot of them always wore boudoir caps when they came down to the stores around nine and ten o'clock to do the buying for the day, and it was a peculiar sight to see them tiptoeing through the back alleyways with a bag of groceries in one hand and their skirts held high with the other.

Toy Shaw ran up to the crowd in the square, pulling out his revolver and pinning his marshal's badge on his shirt at the same time.

"What's all this shooting about?" Toy said, puffing and blowing.

Somebody pointed at the man across the square

against the drug-store brick wall. Nobody remembered ever seeing him before, but he looked a lot like most of the fruit-tree salesmen who came through the country about that time of the year.

"I don't know who did the shooting," the fellow said, "but that's the one who did the running."

"Has he got a gun on him?" Toy asked.

Nobody knew about that. They kept on shaking their heads.

"Well, then," Toy said, putting his gun away and moving his badge to the other side of his shirt. "There's nothing to be scared about."

Just then, when the crowd started to follow Toy over to the drug store, a woman ran down the stairs of the walk-up hotel and dashed into the street.

People everywhere scurried into the buildings. When the barber shop was full, they began crowding into the bank and poolroom.

The woman, who really did not look to be more than an eighteen-year-old girl, had a long-barrel, blue-steel revolver.

Somebody nudged Toy Shaw, and Toy stuck his head out the barber-shop door and ordered her to disarm herself.

"Pitch that gun on the ground, lady," he said, ducking back inside.

The girl leveled the pistol at the wall of the barber

shop and fired it stiff-armed. The pistol recoiled so strongly that she almost toppled over backward. After a while she took her finger out of her ear and looked all around to see if she had hit anybody or anything.

"What's the matter, Toy?" somebody asked him. "You aint scared to disarm a woman, are you?"

Toy pulled up his suspenders and looped them over his shoulders.

"That's one of these gunwomen," he said, keeping back out of sight.

"Shucks, Toy," somebody said, "she's just a girl. She couldn't hit a barn door."

Toy stuck his head through the door once more, and drew it back after he had taken a hasty look outside.

"It's funny the way a woman thinks about a gun before she does anything else when she gets a little peeved about something or other," he said. "It looks like men would've learned by this time that it don't pay to leave firearms laying around where their womenfolks can lay hold of them."

The man across the square had not moved an inch the whole time. He was as motionless as a telephone pole against the drug-store wall.

"What kind of a marshal are you, anyway, Toy," a fellow said, "if you're scared to disarm a woman?"

"I don't remember that being in the bargain," Toy

said. "When I took the oath, it only mentioned armed housebreakers and bank-robbers and other men. It didn't say a single word about gunwomen."

The girl backed across the street, still searching the doorways and windows with her eyes for the man who had run out of the walk-up hotel. When she got to the center of the square, she turned around for the first time and saw the man backed up against the drug-store wall. He looked too scared even to turn and run out of sight.

"Now's your chance, Toy," somebody said, shoving him to the door. "Go on out there and slip up behind on her, and she'll never know what grabbed her."

Toy tried to stay where he was for the present, but the crowd kept on shoving and pushing, and he found himself outside in the street. Somebody slammed the door shut, and unless he turned tail and ran, there was nothing he could do but go in the direction of the girl.

He tiptoed across the street behind her, trying not to make a sound. With every step he took, she took one in the same direction. For a while he did not gain a single inch on her. When she stopped a moment to straighten her stocking, Toy went a little faster.

Just when he was within twenty feet of her, one of the foxhounds that had been asleep under the water-oak tree woke up, scared to death by all the silence around town, and howled.

The girl was as scared as the hound, or Toy, or anyone else. She turned around to see what had happened.

"Don't shoot, lady," Toy begged. "Don't shoot, whatever you do!"

The girl stuck her finger into her ear and fired in Toy's direction. The bullet zipped through the leaves and branches of the tree over his head.

"I never shot at a lady in all my life," Toy said, his voice shaking and thin. "And, lady, I sure don't want to have to do it now."

He pointed at his marshal's badge on his shirt without taking his eyes from her.

"Lady," he said, "whatever you do do, don't shoot that gun again. It's against the ordinance to fire off a gun inside the town limits."

The girl flared up.

"Shut your mouth!" she cried. "Don't you try to tell me what to do!"

Toy glanced behind him to see if any of the crowd was close enough to have heard what she said to him.

"Lady," he said, "I'm just telling you that you're going to have that thing all shot out in another minute or two, and then what are you going to do?"

The girl turned her back on Toy and ran towards the man in front of the drug store. Toy went after her, hoping to be able to stop a murder, if he could get there in plenty of time.

The man was too scared to move an inch, even to save his life. He looked as if he would have given anything he had to be able to run, but it was easy to see that he could not move his feet an inch in any direction.

The girl leveled the gun at the trembling man's chest.

"Don't shoot him!" Toy yelled at her. "Shoot up in the air!"

The girl pointed the gun into the sky and fired the remaining bullets. When the hammer clicked on an empty chamber, she dropped the revolver at her feet.

Toy dashed up and grabbed her around the waist. It looked from the other side of the square as if she sort of swooned in Toy's arms. He had to hold her up when she gave way all at once.

The man sank to the pavement, beads of perspiration jumping like popcorn on his forehead.

By that time the crowd began pouring out of the stores and running across the square.

Toy dragged the girl to the wall beside the white-faced man, and set her down gently. She fainted away again with her head on the man's shoulder.

Somebody ran up and slapped Toy on the back. He jumped to his feet.

"I guess we've got a pretty brave marshal, after all," the fellow said. "There's not many men who would walk right out in broad daylight and disarm a woman."

"It wasn't anything at all," Toy said, standing back and letting the crowd have a chance to look at him. "It was just as simple as falling off a log."

The girl began to regain consciousness. She opened her eyes and shrank in fright when she saw the crowd of strange men all around her. She clutched at the fellow beside her, throwing her arms around his neck and squeezing him tightly to her. The fellow swallowed hard.

"Are you hurt, honey?" she asked him, turning his face to hers with her hands.

The fellow swallowed hard again.

Toy pushed his way through the crowd. The men and boys fell back to let him pass through. When he got past them, he ran his thumbs under his suspender straps and threw them off his shoulders as though they had been belts on a saw-mill engine.

He knew what was coming, and he knew there was nothing he could do to stop it. Somebody followed him a few steps to the corner.

"You'd better hurry home and rest up a while now, Toy," the man said. "I know you must be all wore out after taking a gun away from that thin little girl."

The crowd broke out in laughter. The men were soon so noisy he could not hear anything more that was said to him. He hurried around the corner as fast as he could.

Honeymoon

Honeymoon

NEVER mind what put Claude Barker up to getting married. Nearly everybody does something like that sometime or other. They'll be going along minding their own business for months at a time, and then all at once they come across a girl that sort of oozes when they look at her and . . .

If it had been anybody else than Claude, nobody would have thought much about it. He was one of the bunch that had been hanging around town, mostly at the poolroom, doing nothing most of the time, for five or six years, maybe ten or twelve. Claude said he was waiting for a job at the filling station, but everybody else who wasn't working said that too.

Jack and Crip were sitting in the sun in front of the filling station when Claude went by the first time. That was about ten o'clock that morning, and Claude was on his way to the courthouse to get a license.

"What's Claude up to?" Crip said.

The car Claude had borrowed early that morning from Jack sounded as if it would never make the trip to the courthouse and back.

"Search me," Jack said. "Maybe he thinks he knows where he can find a job."

"Yeah," Crip said, spitting. "But whoever would have thought of borrowing a car to run away from it? If a job ever hears of Claude, it'll wish it hadn't by the time it catches up with him. He'd turn around and fan its tail all the way from here to Atlanta and back again. His old man . . ."

Claude's old man, sitting on the bench in front of the post office, said he thought he knew why Claude had suddenly taken it into his head to get married. Everybody was waiting for the cotton-gin whistle to blow so he could go home to dinner. Claude had been to the courthouse and back, and somebody had seen him drive out to the preacher's house on the edge of town half an hour before.

Claude's old man said he reckoned he knew why Claude was getting married. By God, it wouldn't pain a man much to make a guess like that, somebody said. No, but it would be a bad thing if there were no more girls like Willeen Howard left in the country. That aint no lie. When that time comes, I'll be ready to turn the country over to the niggers and boll weevils and screw-worms and sell out from here.

The ginnery whistle down the railroad tracks blew for the twelve-thirty lay-off. Claude's old man stood up to go home to see what his wife had cooked up for dinner. I'll tell you people what put the marrying bug on Claude. The boy is young yet, and he wasn't used to fooling around with white girls. He's been of the habit . . .

The crowd broke up like a rotten egg hitting the side of a barn.

"Claude's been in the habit . . ."

Old man Barker didn't have time to finish. He had to hurry home and eat his meal before his wife let the victuals get cold.

Downtown at the noon hour was quiet except for a handful of Negroes from the country who were sitting on the shaded railroad-station platform eating rat-trap cheese and soda crackers. Occasionally an automobile would plow through town on its way to Atlanta or Savannah, leaving the air tasting like ant poison for half an hour afterward.

Claude and Willeen came rattling down the street, across the square, Jack's old car hitting the railroad irons with a sound like a brick running through a cotton gin. Claude drove up to the filling station and stopped. Crip woke up and ran out to see who it was. Claude had lifted the seat and was unscrewing the gas-tank cap.

"Boy, you need lots of gas today," Crip said, putting the nozzle into the tank and looking at Willeen at the same time.

"Give me two gallons," Claude said.

"What you two going to do now?" Crip asked, turning the pump crank.

"That aint no lie," Claude said, winking at Willeen.

Crip hung up the hose while Claude was counting out the change for the gasoline. He took a quick look into the back seat to see if Claude and Willeen had any baggage for a trip. There was not a thing. He looked again to be sure. On the floor beside the tire pump and wheel jack he saw a lacy piece of goods with a couple of straps on it that made it look like something or other. He did not have time to find out what. When Jack came back from dinner, Crip could ask him if he had left anything lacy in the back seat of his car.

Crip did not have time to do any more looking around, because he had to have one more look at Willeen before Claude drove off with her. It was too late then to ask her why she had not told him something about it. If he had known about it in time, he could have asked her himself. It would not have been any trouble for him to get married. He could have done it just as easily as Claude did. But, God Almighty, what a funny feeling Willeen gave you when you looked at her real hard. It made you feel as if you were eating a clingstone peach and had got down almost to the last of it, and the more you sucked it, and bit the stone, the better the peach tasted, and you began to feel sort of hoggish but didn't give a damn how you acted when you couldn't get enough of it.

Willeen got back into the front seat and sat down. Claude grabbed up the water bucket and began filling the radiator.

It would have been easy enough to have married her, if you had only thought about it before Claude did. You'd make a monkey of yourself, all over the place, any day of the week, for some of that. By that time your eyes felt dry and stuck in your head when you had blinked them for so long, and when you shut them for a moment to get them moistened, you were ready to start all over again. After that you couldn't help seeing all the pretty things she had and you forgot all about tending the filling station and got to thinking that maybe I could fix it up someway or other. It wasn't so long ago that Willeen told you you could throw her down if you wanted to. You were a damn fool not to do it when she gave you the chance. But that wasn't now by a long shot. WHAT A DAMN FOOL YOU MAKE OF YOURSELF BUT YOU NEVER KNOW IT TILL IT'S TOO LATE.

They drove off down the street leaving Crip standing there looking like a cow mired in quicksand.

Claude drove around the square seven or eight times, warming up the engine, and finally stopped in front of the poolroom. It made him itch all over when he thought of having a cue-stick in his hands. There was no reason why he should not take time to shoot a couple of games. He might be able to win half a dollar, and then he could buy another couple gallons of gas. They could ride twice as far if they had two more.

It was time for the one-thirty ginnery whistle to blow, and people were already on their way back from dinner. A game was just starting when Claude went inside, and he grabbed a cue-stick from the rack and got in. They played five rounds of three-handed straight, and Claude came out even, after all.

Somebody in the street was blowing an automobile horn. Upton Daniels came in, and Claude started a two-handed game of rotation with him. Claude broke, and made the seven- and fifteen-ball.

"Boy, what a shot!" he said. "I wouldn't take dollars for this stick of mine. There's never been one like it before."

Upton made a face by pushing out his mouth.

"You ought to have seen me ring them in last night," said Claude. "Seven and eleven were pay-balls, and I rang them in nine games in a row. It takes a good man to do that."

"Pig's butt," Upton said.

Upton shot and missed an easy one. He banged his

cue-stick on the floor and made another face with his mouth.

Claude ran in three balls, missed the fourth, but Upton was left sewn up behind the fourteen. Upton jerked up his cue and scattered the balls with the heavy end.

"That gives a man away every time," Claude said, chalking his cue-tip. "The first thing I learned about shooting pool was to keep my head. That's why I'm the best shot in town. If you was as good as I am, you could make yourself a little money now and then off the drummers who come to town. I know you've made runs of thirty-seven and thirty-eight every once in a while, but that was just luck."

"Pig's butt," Upton said.

The horn out in the street started blowing again. When they finished the game, Claude went out to the front of the poolroom and looked into the street to see who was making so much racket. He had missed a couple of easy shots just on that account.

When he saw Willeen sitting in the car, he shoved his cue-stick at Upton and ran outside. Willeen looked angry.

"God Almighty," Claude said under his breath, getting into the car and driving off.

It was about five o'clock in the afternoon then, and

there were only two gallons of gasoline in the tank. Ten miles out of town, Claude turned around and came back. When they reached his house, it was time for supper.

"I'll go inside and fix things up first," he told Willeen. "It won't take long."

He got out and started up the steps. Willeen called him back, and he went to the car.

"I'd like to go home first and get a few things, Claude," she said. "You wouldn't mind, would you?"

"Sure, that's all right," he said, starting the car. "By the time you're ready, I'll have got things fixed up here. I'll be by for you about ten o'clock."

"You don't have to wait that long, Claude," Willeen said. "I'll be ready in just a few minutes."

"I've got to see a fellow downtown," Claude said. "It might take me a couple of hours to find him. We'd better make it ten o'clock, like I said. I've got to take this car back where I got it from, for another thing."

On his way back after leaving Willeen at her father's house, Claude stopped at the poolroom a minute. Somebody gave him a drink of corn, and after that he decided to shoot a few games of pool with Upton before going home to fix things up for Willeen.

Claude's old man was downtown early the next

morning. When he passed the filling station, Jack and Crip asked him where Claude was.

"He and Willeen are still asleep," Claude's old man said. "But I reckon you'll be seeing Claude most anytime now. Is there anything in particular you boys want to see him about? Is that job ready for him?"

"He's still got my car," Jack said. "He ought to bring it back. I only let him have it for a couple hours yesterday, and he kept it all day and all night."

"Don't worry about your car, son," old man Barker said. "It's standing up there in the front yard of the house right this minute. Claude'll be coming downtown with it before very long."

He went across the square and sat down in the shade in front of the post office. There were three or four men over there who had been talking about the news in the morning paper.

After he had sat down, somebody asked him how Claude was getting along now that he was married to Willeen Howard. Old man Barker nodded his head. Somebody else spat into the dust. This would sure God be a puny country if it got cleaned out of girls like that. If the time ever comes when they don't invite a throw-down, then it's time to let the niggers and boll weevils and screw-worms run wild. Claude's old man sort of chuckled to himself. The boy wasn't up when he left home. What did Claude have to say when he woke up this morning? I'll bet it was the same thing I said when I was in his place once, the fellow said, winking.

About an hour later Claude drove Jack's car down to the filling station. They were waiting for him.

"How's everything, Claude?" Jack said.

"Couldn't be better," Claude told him.

"It's a funny feeling, though, I bet," Jack said.

Claude turned and looked at Crip a moment. Crip looked straight at him, but he had nothing to say to Claude.

"Funny?" Claude said, laughing a little and going to the gas pump and leaning against it. "Funny aint no name for it, Crip."

Crip looked at him between the eyes.

"I still can't seem to get over it somehow. This morning I woke up and opened my eyes and I saw a bare arm lying over me. When I saw it, I was scared to death. I jumped out of bed in a hurry, thinking to myself, 'What in hell am I doing sleeping in bed with a white girl?' "

Crip kicked at the tires on Jack's old car to see how well they were holding up. He walked all the way around it a couple times. Nobody had said anything after Claude finished talking.

After a while Claude walked off down the street towards the poolroom. Jack pushed the car behind the filling station where it would be out of the way. While he was back there, he took the cap off the gas tank to see if Claude had left any gas in it. There was almost a whole gallon inside. Jack thought that was funny, because Claude had started off into the country as if he had figured on taking a trip somewhere.

Martha Jean

Martha Jean

WE HAD got booted out of a flat in the West End where we had caught up with one of the floating crap games and, instead of making the rounds on a raw night like that, we took a short cut across town to Nick's Place. Sleet was falling, and the wind was as sharp as knife-blades. We met two or three men on the way; everybody was bent almost double against the icy wind, holding his hat and coat with numb fingers.

"What did you let them throw us out for, Hal?" the Type said. "There's no law against a man following a public crap game. I've gone broke in better flats than that one, anyway."

The Type bumped into a lamp post. He turned around and kicked the iron pole with his foot.

"Winter's a hell of a time of year," he said. "Let's go home."

"Nick's Place will be heated up," I said. "Come on, and we'll look in there for a while."

The usual after-supper crowd was standing around the stove in Nick's Place, warming their fingers against the red-hot sides of the blast heater. Como, the Negro porter, stoked the fire and kept his back turned on the sleet that slashed against the door and windows.

When the Type and I walked in, Nick ran up from somewhere and met us half-way.

"I'm going to close up early tonight," Nick said. "You boys will have to go home for a change. Won't your folks be surprised to see you, though?"

"You mean you're telling us to get out?" the Type said.

"There's no money in keeping open on a night like this," Nick argued. "I'd just be wasting heat and light, and getting nowhere at all."

"Hello, Nick," I said. "How about lending me a dollar till sometime next week? Here's how it is. I started out—"

"No loans tonight, boys," he said. "I'm going to close up right away."

Como shivered.

"If it's all the same to you, Mr. Nick," Como said, "I'd just as lief stay and sleep right here on the floor by the stove tonight. Way out where I live, my old woman—"

"And burn up half a ton of coal," Nick said.

"I won't burn but one little shovelful the whole night long," Como pleaded. "A black man like me would die of pneumonia if I had to go out in that cold sleet tonight."

"You drag yourself out of here in half an hour, Como," Nick told him. "After you sweep out, I don't care where you go. You can go home if you want to."

The crowd around the stove pressed a little closer at the prospect of having to leave a warm room.

Nick came around the stove behind me. He shoved his thumb into my ribs.

"Wake up, Hal," he said. "What's the matter with you? Broke again? No drinks, no eats, no playing the machines?"

"I'm cleaned out tonight, Nick," I told him. "If I hadn't got kicked out of a game over in the West End, I'd have been on my feet."

Nick shrugged his shoulders and walked over to the wall where the row of slot machines stood on the tables. He shoved his fingers into the cups at the bottom of the machines where sometimes he found a nickel or a quarter somebody left behind.

"You boys are pretty bum sports," Nick said, coming back to the stove. "Why don't you go out and raise some money to play the machines with? The Type hasn't had a dime in his pocket this week."

"What's the matter with you, Nick?" the Type said. "What do you want me to do? Go out and crack the First National Bank?"

"I'm carrying you for six dollars now," Nick said. "I've got to have a pay day soon."

"I'll see what I can do," the Type told him.

Como was dumping a scuttle of coal into the stove when the front door burst open in a whirl of sleet and icy air. Everybody turned and looked in that direction just as a girl's head was seen outside. She stepped into the doorway.

"Shut that door," Nick said.

Como ran to the front and closed the door.

Everybody looked surprised at the sight of a girl in Nick's Place. I had never seen one there before; I had never heard of a girl entering the place. Nick's was a hangout for men and boys, and there was nothing there except the slot machines and pool tables. The lunch counter was hardly a place to come for a meal. Nick and Como had drinks and a few sandwiches, but that was all.

The forlorn-looking girl stood at the front of the room, shivering a little. The sleet on her hair and coat began to melt in the warm air, but her slippers were wet.

"Who's that?" the Type said. "She doesn't look like one of the girls around the corner to me. I never saw her before."

Como came back and dumped another scuttleful of coal into the iron heater. It was red-hot all over.

"I'll bet she ran away from home," the Type said.

Nick had gone up to the girl, and he was looking

at her closely. She drew away from him, and he had to go and stand with his back against the door to keep her from running out into the street.

"This is a hell of a place for a runaway country girl to land," the Type said.

"She won't stay in here long," I said. "As soon as she sees what she's got into, she'll leave."

The Type looked at the faces in the crowd around the stove.

"I'd hate to see . . ."

Nick said something to the girl, and the Type stopped to hear what it was.

"If anybody starts getting fresh with her," I said, "I'm going to start swinging. I'm not going to stay here and see her get ganged."

The Type did not pay any attention to what I had said. He walked a little closer to the front in order to hear what Nick was saying to her.

The girl found her handkerchief and wiped the tears that sprang into her eyes.

"What do you want?" Nick said.

She shook her head.

"What did you come in here for if you don't want anything?" Nick asked her. "What's up?"

She shook her head again. She was a girl about fifteen or sixteen, and a lot prettier than any of the girls in the house around the corner. To look at her reminded you of the girls you had seen going to Sunday school on Sunday mornings.

"Hungry?" Nick asked her.

She made no reply, but it was easy to see that she had come in for something to eat, thinking that Nick's Place was a café.

"Como," Nick yelled, "bring us up some coffee and a couple of sandwiches. Get a hump on!"

"Yes, sir!" Como said, patting the warmth of the stove before hurrying to the lunch counter.

Nick led the girl to the counter and made her sit down on one of the stools. He sat down beside her, between her and the door.

The boys around the stove began winking at each other, nodding their heads at Nick and the girl.

When Como had the coffee hot, Nick asked her what her name was.

"Martha Jean," she said without hesitation.

Nick sat a little closer.

"Where you live?"

Martha Jean shook her head, tears springing to her eyes once more. Nick was satisfied. He did not ask her any more questions.

"When she finishes, give her a slice of cake, Como," Nick said, getting up.

Como shook his head.

"There aint no cake, Mr. Nick," Como said.

Nick flared up.

"I said give her cake, Como, you shoe-shine African!" he shouted. "When I say give her cake, I mean give it to her!"

"Yes, sir, boss!" Como said, shaking his head.

Nick came over towards the stove, walking sideways while he tried to keep his eyes on Martha Jean, and washing his hands in the air. When he got to the stove, he looked the crowd over, and picked on the Type to glare at as usual.

"All right now, you boys beat it somewhere else. Go on home, or somewhere. I'm closing up for the night."

Nobody made a move to leave.

Nick shoved the Type away from the stove.

"The next time you come back, have that six dollars you owe me," Nick told him, pushing.

"What the hell, Nick?" the Type said. "You've never hurried me for anything on the books like this before. What's the matter with you?"

"I had a bad dream last night," Nick said. "I dreamed that they hauled you off to a big stone-wall building and you got electrocuted. I've got to look out for myself now."

Some of the crowd moved away from the stove, but nobody left the room.

Nick shoved me with a stiff-arm.

"What's the big hurry, Nick?" I said to him.

"That's my business," Nick said. "Get a hump on."

"When is the girl going?"

"Martha Jean's staying."

"You can't do that, Nick," I said. "She came in here to get something to eat. She's nothing to me, but I hate to see her get pushed about like one of the girls around the corner."

"You're going to talk yourself out of a good thing, Hal," he said. "Don't I lend you money every time you ask for it, almost? Don't I keep you posted on the lay of the land? Don't I bail your brother-in-law every time he's picked up? What's the matter with you?"

Nick shoved me again, harder than before.

"What are you going to do with her?" I said.

"That's Nick's business," he answered. "If you know what's good for you, Hal, you'll get out of here before you talk too much."

The rest of the crowd was standing around the door, watching the girl. The Type was buttoning up his coat to leave.

Nick shoved me with his stiff-arm again.

"When you get home tonight, Hal," he said, pushing and shoving me towards the door, "tell your folks to give you something to do if they're not going to give you any spending money. I can't be having you hanging around my place if you don't have any money to play the machines with."

Nick turned his back on me and went over to where the girl was seated at the counter. She had finished eating, and Nick took her arm and pulled her towards the stove. She tried to pull away from him, but during all that time she had not raised her eyes to look at anybody in the room.

He dragged her to the stove.

"Cold, Martha Jean?" he asked her, putting his arms around her.

Some of the crowd had already left. Nearly all the fellows were letting Nick drive them out because they were afraid he would stop making loans when they were broke. Besides that, there were the tips Nick was always passing out when he got news of a sure thing to bet on. If Nick stopped letting us in on sure things, nearly everybody would stop getting spending money. Nick always got it all back, sooner or later, in the slot machines. Nick's crowd was afraid not to do what he told them to do.

The Type and myself stood at the door watching Nick and Martha Jean at the stove.

"Got a place to stay tonight?" he asked her.

She answered him with a shake of her head and with a shiver that convulsed her whole body.

"How long have you been in town?" he asked.

"I came today," Martha Jean said.

"Looking for a job?"

"Yes."

Nick squeezed her with his arm.

"You don't have to worry about that any more," he told her, trying to raise her face up to his. "I'll fix everything for you."

Martha Jean tried again to get away from him, but Nick put both arms around her and held her tight to his side.

"Como," Nick said, "go upstairs and fix a place for Martha Jean. Fix up the front room for her, the one with the new bed and chairs in it. Get a hump on!"

"Yes, sir, boss!" Como said, tapping the red-hot stove with his fingers.

Martha Jean looked up for the first time. There was a startled expression in her eyes. When she turned towards the Type and me, I could not keep from going to her. She looked as helpless as a rabbit that had been caught in a steel trap for two or three days.

Nick turned around and glared at me.

Como could be heard stamping around upstairs in the room overhead. He was fixing things in a hurry so he could get back downstairs to the red-hot stove.

"Do you want to stay here with him?" I said to her, edging closer. "Or do you want to leave?"

Martha Jean started to say something. Her tears

began flowing again, and she fought Nick desperately.

"What did I tell you, Hal?" Nick said angrily. "You wouldn't believe me, would you?"

He turned around and shook his head at me.

"Didn't I tell you you'd talk yourself out of a good thing? You wouldn't believe me, would you?"

He turned the girl loose for a moment, and swung around on his heels. Before I had a chance to duck, his fist flew at my head. The next thing I knew I was on the floor, unable to tell which was up and which was downside.

I could not see what the Type was doing, but I knew he was not helping me. Nick went back to Martha Jean, unbuttoning her coat and putting his arms under it. He held her so tight that she cried with pain.

By the time I could get to my feet, I did not know what to do next. After Nick had knocked me down, I began to realize there was nothing I could do to stop him. If the Type had helped me, it would have turned out differently. But the Type was thinking about Nick's loans and race-track tips. He stood at the door ready to leave.

When I was on both feet again, Nick stepped over and shoved me towards the door with his stiff-arm. I went flying across the room, falling against the Type.

The Type opened the door and tried to push me out into the street.

I fought him off and came back inside the door.

Nick picked up Martha Jean and started for the stairway with her. She began to scratch and fight, and Nick had a hard time keeping her from hurting him. She finally succeeded in scratching his face with her fingernails, and Nick dropped her like a hot brick.

"Como!" he yelled.

Como came tumbling down the stairs.

"Put him out and lock the door, Como," Nick ordered. "Throw him out, if he won't get out."

Nick grabbed Martha Jean again. She was such a little girl, and so young, she did not have much chance with Nick. All he had to do to hold her was to lock one arm around her neck, and cover both her hands with his other one.

Como picked up the iron stove-poker and came towards me. He was scared to death. I knew he would never hit me, but I could see that he was so scared of Nick that he had to pretend to be trying to drive me out the door. The Type had gone.

"Throw that poker down, Como," I said.

"Mr. Hal," Como said, "you'd better leave Mr. Nick alone when he's mad. There aint no telling what he's liable to do when he gets good and mad at you."

"Shut up, Como," I said.

Nick picked Martha Jean up once more and carried her as far as the stairway. There he put her down quickly and ran towards me. I tried to meet him with my fists, but he jumped up into the air and came down on top of me. My bones felt as if they were being crushed like eggshells. When I woke up, I was lying on my face on the icy pavement.

The door was locked, and all but one light downstairs had been turned off. In the rear of the room, under one light, I could see Como throwing a hod of coal into the stove and trying to see through the window to the street outside at the same time.

I crossed the street, shielding my face against the sleet and wind that raced down the street. While I waited, I called for the Type two or three times. He did not answer, and I knew he had gone. There was nobody else on the street on a night like that.

Upstairs in the room Como had opened up, Nick had taken off his coat and was trying to make Martha Jean take off hers. She ran from him, from one side of the room to the other. Nick finally gave up trying to catch her, and picked up his coat and swung it at her.

At first she tried to cover her face and head against the stinging blows of the coat, but when Nick struck her across the back with it, she fell on the floor. All I could see was Nick bending over her and picking her up. When she was on her feet again, she got away from him. Nick swung at her with his coat, and struck the electric-light bulb hanging on a cord from the ceiling. The room suddenly became as black as the night outside.

I stood shaking and trembling in the street. The stinging, whipping, cutting sleet and wind blinded my eyes, and it was hard to open them after the light in the room went out. After a while, when Como had put out the last light downstairs, I turned and walked heavily up the street.

Once I thought I heard Martha Jean scream, but when I stopped and listened in the stinging sleet, I could not hear it again. After that I did not know whether it was she or whether it was only the wind that cried against the sharp corners of the buildings.

A Day's Wooing

A Day's Wooing

WHEN Tuffy Webb woke up that morning, the first thing he saw was his new straw hat hanging on the back of the cane-bottomed chair beside the bed. The red, orange, and blue silk band around the hat looked as bright in the sunshine as the decorations in the store windows in town on circus day. He reached out and felt the rough crown and brim, running his fingers over the stiff brown straw. He would never have to step aside for anybody, in a hat like that. That was all he needed, to get the world by the tail.

"Maybe that won't knock a few eyes out!" Tuffy said, throwing off the covers and leaping to the floor. "They'll all be cross-eyed from looking at it."

He placed the hat carefully on his head and walked over to the mirror on the wall. The new straw hat looked even finer Sunday morning than it had Saturday night, when he tried it on in the store.

"When Nancy sees this lid, she'll come tumbling," Tuffy said, stepping back and tilting the hat a little on one side of his head and winking at himself under the brim.

He walked past the mirror several times, free and easy in his loose knee-length nightshirt, turning his eyes to see himself in passing. It was easy to get up courage in a hat like that.

"I could have all the girls after me now if I wanted them," he said to himself.

Tuffy got dressed in a hurry and made a fire in the cookstove. He pulled the hat down carefully over his head so it would not fall off and hit the floor while he was cooking breakfast.

During all the time he was in the kitchen he kept thinking to himself that he would not have to keep bach much longer after that, not after Nancy saw him in his new hat. She would be tickled to death to marry him now, the first time she saw him walking up to her house with the straw sailor tilted over one ear, sort of like a cock's comb that always looked like it was going to fall off but never did.

After breakfast Tuffy had to drive the cows to the pasture on the other side of the creek because it had become time for them to have a change of feed, and the johnson grass over there was ready for grazing.

He started off with his hat on his head, but he got to thinking about it and finally decided he ought to leave it at the house. Sometimes a yearling took to heels and bolted off into a thicket, and he did not like to think of taking any chances of having the hat fall off into the briers and mud, and maybe being trampled by the cows. Now that he was thinking about it, he remembered seeing a cow chew up a straw hat once and swallow it.

He hurried back to the house and hung the hat on the cane-bottomed chair beside the bed.

Tuffy got back from the pasture at about eleven o'clock, and he changed his clothes right away, putting on his coat and the hat. After that he still had almost an hour to wait before he could leave home, because he did not wish to get to the Millers' while they were eating dinner. If he did that, one of the Millers would be certain to say that he had got there then to get something to eat.

He walked out on the porch and leaned against the railing for a while. The sun was almost directly overhead, and there was not a cloud in sight. He knew he could not have chosen a finer day to go calling on Nancy in a new straw hat. There was not a single drop of rain in the whole sky above.

"This would be a dandy time to speak to Nancy about us getting married," he said, going out into the yard and walking first around the chinaberry tree and then around the willow. "All I'd have to do would be to ask her, and I know already what Nancy'll say. She's just as willing as I am, and she knows it. It wouldn't do her any good to try to show otherwise."

Tuffy leaned against the willow, picking at the bark with his thumbnail.

"If I go right up to her and say, 'Nancy, how about me and you hitching up together?' she'll say, 'When, Tuffy?' and I'll say, 'The sooner the better suits me.' Then she'll say, 'Nothing would please me more.' That's all there will be to it, and it'll be all planned and settled. All I'll have to do is get a preacher to marry us, and then me and Nancy'll be married for a fare-you-well. Getting married wouldn't take long, maybe no longer than tomorrow noon. We'll probably start right in tomorrow some time. That's none too soon for me, and I know it won't be none too soon for Nancy."

Tuffy went over and sat on the woodpile.

"I'll go over there to old Berry Miller's and walk right up to where they're all sitting on the porch and lose no time about it. Berry'll probably want to know what I came for, all dressed up like this in a coat and a new straw hat, and I'll soon tell him, too. 'Well,' I'll say, 'I came to marry Nancy, Berry. How do you like that? Me and her are getting married right off.' He won't scare me a bit, no matter what he says. He might have some little fault to find to begin with, but there's no objection I know about that's good enough to stop me from going ahead and getting married to Nancy. I'll walk right up to where she's sitting on the porch and put my arm around her and show those Millers I mean business and don't mean maybe."

Tuffy picked up a piece of stovewood and began tearing splinters out of it with his fingernails. He piled the splinters in a little stack between his feet.

"If old Berry Miller makes any show of getting his bristles up, I'll reach right down and kiss her in front of all the Millers, and then pick her up and walk off with her without so much as looking back at them even once. That'll show Berry that when I set out to get married, I don't let nothing in the whole wide world stop me. Those Millers can't put the scare into me."

He hurled the stick of stovewood across the yard. It narrowly missed hitting one of his hens asleep in a dust hole under the chinaberry tree. The hen woke up and ran squawking for her life. The other chickens got scared and followed her under the house.

Tuffy took out his handkerchief and wiped the sweatband of his new straw hat. It was a scorching hot day, especially out in the sun at midday, and the heavy wool coat had never felt so tight before.

"If I had thought to get the license yesterday, me and Nancy could have got married today," he said disgustedly, kicking at the ground. "Now, why didn't I think about that yesterday? I'll have to wait till tomorrow before I can go to the courthouse now."

He got up and walked to his car. He had not intended getting inside, because it was still about half an hour too soon for him to leave, but he could not wait any longer. He would have to drive around ten or fifteen miles an hour, and maybe stop at the creek and wait a while, but he was too anxious to be on his way to Nancy's house to wait around home any longer. He started the car and drove off, pushing the new straw hat tightly on his head so the wind could not blow it off.

It was half past twelve o'clock when Tuffy Webb drove up to the Berry Miller place and stopped his car in the shade. He had not got there a minute too soon, because the Millers were at that minute coming out on the porch from the dinner table. It was getting hotter all the time, and Tuffy sat in his car for several minutes trying to cool off before getting out and going up to the house.

Before looking at the Millers on the porch, he took out his handkerchief and tried to wipe off some of the perspiration that trickled down his cheeks and down the back of his neck. When he finished, he took off his hat and wiped the sweatband good and dry.

Old man Berry Miller waved at him from the porch. One of the Miller boys rose up on his elbow from the porch floor to see what Tuffy was doing.

Tuffy got out and walked stiff and erect across the

yard to the house. He was uncomfortable all over, and it made his face flush red when he realized what he was doing there. The Millers had a way of staring at him that made him forget what he was doing sometimes.

"Come on in on the porch out of that hot sun and have a slice of watermelon fresh out of the bottom of the well," Berry Miller said. "There's not much left, but what there is, you're welcome to it. It's only the leavings."

Berry brushed away the flies with his hat. They swarmed around the porch for a few moments and then settled back again on the rinds and watermelon seed scattered about on the floor.

"Well, howdy, folks," Tuffy said.

One of the boys waved his arm at Tuffy, and both the girls giggled. Berry's wife rocked back and forth in her chair without saying a thing. A watermelon seed had stuck to her chin and was drying there. Tuffy wondered why nobody told her to brush it off.

"Mighty hot day today," he said, flushing red again when his eyes swept the porch and saw the two girls.

Their white dresses were starched so stiffly that they looked as if corset stays had been sewn into the cloth.

"Sort of," Berry said. "Can't complain, though. Heat's due us."

The boys on the other end of the porch sat up.

"What are you all dressed up for, Tuffy?" Henry asked him. "Going somewhere?"

Tuffy's eyes dropped and he dug the toe of his shoe into the sandy yard.

Nancy, the oldest girl, giggled again.

Tuffy looked up quickly, hoping to see her plain.

"You're dressed up fit to kill, aint you, Tuffy?" Henry said.

Berry kicked a piece of watermelon rind off the porch.

"That's a mighty fine-looking straw hat you've got on there, Tuffy," Berry said. "You must have bought that at a store somewhere, and paid a lot of money for it, in the bargain. A pretty all-colored band like that don't come on everyday hats."

Tuffy nodded his head.

The other Miller boy on the porch, Clyde, scraped up a handful of watermelon seed and began shooting them between his fingers. Presently one of the seed hit Tuffy in the face, making him jump as if somebody had taken a slingshot and hit him in the eye with a hickory nut. Tuffy would not look at Clyde, because he and Clyde never had got along any too well. They had had several fist fights already that summer.

Berry's wife moved to and fro in her rocker, looking disinterestedly at Tuffy. The watermelon seed had dried on her chin and was stuck there for good. He glanced at her, and their eyes met. Whenever she looked at him, it always made Tuffy feel as if she were looking at some object directly behind him. She had never spoken a word to him in all her life.

Nancy smoothed out the skirt of her starched white dress, bending the stiff hem down over her knees. He could still see where her stockings ended on her legs. Nancy's sister looked at Tuffy and giggled.

"I just thought I'd drop by," Tuffy said at last. "I didn't have much else to do today."

"Had any watermelon today so far?" Berry asked him.

"No," Tuffy said.

"If you don't mind eating the leavings," Berry said, waving his hand at the rind-strewn porch, "you're welcome to have some."

Tuffy looked to see what Nancy was doing, but he could not see the expression on her face when his eyes were watching the black and white garter-line on her legs. She bent the starched hem over again, but when she leaned back, it straightened out again and her legs above the stocking tops were as bold as ever.

"Aint you staying?" Berry asked.

"I don't care if I do," Tuffy said. "I was just riding around, and I thought I'd stop by."

Clyde picked up a piece of rind and threw it at the tree in the yard.

"It's been quite a while since I last saw you all dressed up like that," Berry said. "If I remember correctly, the last time was at the baptizing over at the church about a month ago. Wasn't you all dressed up that day, Tuffy?"

Nancy giggled and hid her face against her sister's shoulder. Tuffy blushed again.

"I didn't have this new hat then, though," he said.

"So you didn't!" Berry said. "That is right, aint it? That hat looks so natural on your head that I forgot all about it. But you did have on a coat that day, didn't you?"

Tuffy nodded, digging the toe of his shoe into the yard.

"I wish you had come by a little sooner," Berry said. "It's pretty late now to get any of the good part of the melons. The leavings aint much to offer a body. But of course, now, if you aint particular, just go ahead and help yourself."

One of the boys kicked a piece of rind across the porch and it fell into the yard near Tuffy's feet. He looked at it, all covered with sand.

"Where you going, Tuffy?" Henry asked him.

"Nowhere much," Tuffy said.

"How about me and you going off a piece?" Henry said, winking. "There's some easy pickings on Sunday afternoons over beyond Hardpan."

Tuffy glanced at Nancy. There was a peculiar look on her face that made him uneasy. The garter-line on her legs wavered in his sight when she rocked slightly in her chair. He dropped his eyes to the ground once more.

"I don't reckon I can right now," he told Henry, blushing red all over.

The two girls began whispering to each other. Every once in a while Nancy glanced up at Tuffy, and then she quickly looked the other way.

Tuffy took off his hat and fanned his face with it.

"It's about time to do some thinking about a little foxhunting, aint it, Tuffy?" Berry said. "These nights now are beginning to have a little nip in them, along about midnight, and the foxes will be running before you know it. Anyway, it don't hurt none to sort of warm up the hounds. They've been laying around here all summer and have got as lazy as can be. I been thinking lately of going out some night pretty soon and giving them a short run."

Tuffy nodded his head, but he did not say anything.

"I been thinking about making a trade of some kind for a couple more hunters," Berry said. "That Blackie is still a little lame from last year, and that Elsie is weighted down with pups. That Rastus looks like he takes to cold-trailing more and more every year, and I'm a little upset. I don't reckon it would do any harm to make a trade of some kind, if I could find exactly what I'm looking for. I've got a mule that's stove-up pretty bad, and I figure I need hunting dogs a lot more now than I do a blamed stiff-legged mule."

Tuffy glanced up at Nancy, looking as if he were bursting with something to say. He looked at her so desperately that she reached over and bent the starched hem and held it down. He could do no more than swallow hard and flush red all over. It made his skin feel prickly under the heavy coat when she looked at him.

Clyde sat up and slid down to the edge of the porch. He sat swinging his legs over the edge and looking at Tuffy. Tuffy was becoming more and more uncomfortable. He had been standing for half an hour in the hot sun, and he caught himself swaying on his feet.

"I sure admire that new straw hat of yours, Tuffy," Berry said. "Especially that all-colored pretty band around it."

Tuffy looked desperately at Nancy, and then glanced at the rest of the family. Everyone, except Nancy, stared right back at him. Nancy hung her head when their eyes met.

Henry crossed the yard between him and the house, taking something out of his pocket. He began pulling on it, making it snap like elastic. When he stopped in front of Tuffy, Tuffy looked to see what Henry was playing with. It was a girl's garter, bouna in pink silk, and tied in a bow with a red rosebud sewn into it. Tuffy jumped as if he had been pricked with a pin.

Tuffy backed off, taking short steps towards his car.

"Not going so soon?" Berry said. "Why, it hardly seems like more than a minute ago when you got here."

Tuffy stopped. Henry had kept up with him, snapping the garter. He put one end against Tuffy's arm, pulled the other end back a foot or two, and turned it loose. Tuffy jumped when the elastic stung him.

"Where you going, Tuffy?" Henry asked him.

Tuffy looked at the porch where Nancy was. She had sat upright in the chair, leaning slightly forward, and stopped rocking. The starched flare of her skirt had straightened out once more, and he was glad she wore yellow garters.

He started backing away again. Henry followed him, springing the elastic rosebud-trimmed garter at him.

"Let's me and you ride over beyond Hardpan, Tuffy," Henry urged. "It won't be no trouble at all to find us a couple of girls, and we can make a lot of headway on a Sunday afternoon. How about it, Tuffy, huh?"

Tuffy backed away faster, shaking his head. When

he got to the tree where his car was, he turned around and jumped into the front seat.

Nancy ran into the house. She could be heard crying all the way to the back porch.

When Tuffy got his car started, Berry got up and walked out into the yard. He watched the automobile disappear over the hill, trying to turn his ear away from Henry's cursing.

"I hate to see a man rush off like that," Berry said. "I'd have swore he came here for some purpose to begin with."

He stood with his back to the house while Clyde left the porch and crossed the field to get some more watermelons to cool in the bottom of the well.

The Cold Winter

The Cold Winter

AFTER I had been in town a week, I began going early in the evening to the room I had rented, to lie awake under the warmth of the blanket.

Out on the streets, when night fell, it was always cold. There was usually a chill wet wind from the river, and from the bare uplands the February winter descended hour after hour, freezing and raw. Even men with overcoats hurried through the icy streets with lowered heads fighting the cold, hurrying towards heated homes.

It was cold in the unheated room I had rented, but the warmth of the blanket was like the clinging arms of a girl.

By the third night of the week I had got accustomed to the unheated house. At first I could not sleep. But on that evening I took off my shoes as soon as I had reached the room and got into bed immediately. For the next five or six hours I lay awake, warm under the blanket, while frost on the window-panes formed slowly and precisely into fragile designs of cold beauty.

Out in the hall I could hear people passing quickly

from room to room, hurrying through the cold corridor while the contracted boards of the floor creaked under their feet.

After a while I became conscious of warm air flowing through the cracks in the wall. A young woman and her small daughter lived in the room next to mine, on the right, and the heat they had was escaping into my room. I could smell the scorched air and the burned gas of their heater. I lay awake then, listening to the movements in the next room, while their slowly formed picture was melted into my memory. Towards midnight I fell asleep, remembering only that in the next room the young woman moved lightly when she walked and that the small girl spoke to her mother softly and lovingly.

After that night I began coming home much earlier in the evening to cover myself with the warmth of the blanket and to lie awake in the darkness listening to all that happened in the next-door room. The young woman prepared supper for the girl and herself, and then they sat at the small table by the window and ate slowly, laughing and talking. The little girl was about eight, and her mother was almost as young as she when they laughed and talked.

The cold of the unheated room was not so hard to bear as it had been before I came to know them.

I knew by the end of that second week how each

of them looked even though I had never seen either of them. Through the thin plaster wall I could hear everything they said and did, and I followed the motions of their hands and the expressions on their faces from second to second, hour after hour. The young woman was not working, either; she remained in the room most of the day, going out only in the morning for half an hour to walk with the girl to school, and again in the afternoon to walk home with her. The rest of the day she sat in the room, by the window, looking out over the red-painted tin roof across the way, and waiting for mid-afternoon to come so she could walk to the school for her daughter.

There were other people in the house, many of them. The three floors of the building were rented, room by room, to men and women who came and went during all hours. Some of them worked during the day, some at night, and many had no jobs at all. But even though there were many people in the house, no one ever came to my door, and no one ever went to the young woman's door next to mine. Sometimes there would be the sound of a man walking heavily, coming hurriedly down the hall, and the young woman would jump from her chair by the window and run frantically to the door, leaning against it while her fingers held the key in the lock and listening to the sound of the man's stride. After he had passed, she went slowly back to her chair and sat down once more to look out over the red-painted tin roof across the way.

Into the month of February it became colder and colder, but I was warm when I lay under the blanket and listened to the sounds that came through the thin plaster wall.

It was not until I had become aware of her running to the door each time the sound of a man's footstep rang through the rooms that I realized something was about to happen. I did not know what the happening was to be, nor when, but each morning before leaving my room I waited and listened for several minutes to hear if she were standing against her door or sitting in her chair. When I came back in the evening, I pressed my ear against the cold wall to listen again.

That evening, after I had listened for nearly half an hour, I knew something was about to happen; and for the first time in my life, while I stood there shivering in the cold, I had the desire to be the father of a child. I did not stop to turn on the light, but climbed straightway into bed without even taking off my shoes. I lay tensely awake upon the bed for a long time listening to the movements on the other side of the wall. The young woman was quick and nervous, and her face was white and drawn. The little girl was put to bed as soon as they had finished eating supper and, without a word being spoken, the young woman went to her chair by the window to sit and wait. She sat silently, not even rocking, for a long time. I had raised my head from the pillow, and my neck was stiff and cold after the strain of holding my head horizontally without support.

The desire to be the father of a child left me in a daze. No woman could be the mother until I was the father, and I realized only then that I was he.

It was eleven o'clock before I heard another sound in the room next to mine. During the three hours that I had lain awake on the bed waiting, she had not moved from her chair. But at eleven o'clock she got up and drank a glass of water and covered the girl with another blanket. When she had finished, she moved to her chair for a moment, and then she carried it to the door and sat down. She sat and waited. Before another hour had passed, a man came down the hall, walking heavily on the contracted boards of the floor. We both heard him coming, and we both jumped to our feet. I ran to the wall and pressed my ear against the cold white plaster and waited. The young woman leaned against the door, her fingers gripped around the key, and listened with bated breath. The little girl was sound asleep in bed.

After I had been standing for several minutes I felt

the cold of the unheated room wither my hands and feet. Under the warmth of the blanket I had forgotten how cold it was, and the blood had raced through me while I waited still and tense and listened to the sounds in the building. But standing in the unheated room, with my face and ear pressed against the cold white plaster, I was shaking as though with a chill.

The man came to the door next to mine and stopped. I could hear the woman's trembling, and the breathing that jerked her body, and each moment I expected to hear her scream.

He knocked on the door once and waited. She did not open it. He turned the knob and shook it. She pressed with all her strength against the door, and held the key in its place with fingers of steel.

"I know you are in there, Eloise," he said slowly; "open the door and let me in."

She made no reply. I could hear through the thin wall the strain of her body against the frail door.

"I'm coming in," he said.

He had barely finished before there was a sudden thrust of his shoulder against the door that burst the lock and threw him inside. Even then there was no sound from her lips. She ran to the bed and threw herself upon it, hugging desperately in her arms the girl who had slept so soundly. I who would be the father shivered and waited.

"I didn't come here to argue with you," the man said. "I came here to put an end to this mess. Get up off the bed."

It was then for the first time that evening that I heard the sound of the young woman's voice. She had sprung to her feet and was facing him. I who would be the father pressed my face and ear against the cold white plaster and waited.

"She's as much mine as she is yours. You can't take her away from me."

"You took her away from me, didn't you? Well, it's my turn now. I'm her father."

"Henry!" she begged. "Henry, please don't!"

"Shut up," he said.

He strode to the bed and lifted the girl in his arms.

"I'll kill you, Henry, if you take her out of this room," she said slowly. "I mean that, Henry."

He walked with the girl to the door and stopped. He was not excited, and his breath was not even audible through the thin wall. But the woman was frantic; she was the mother. I who would be the father was helpless; my hands and feet were numbed with the cold and I could not move the muscles of my lips. The young woman had not begun to cry, but through the plaster wall I could hear her breathe, and I could feel the quick movements of her body.

He turned around.

"You'll do what?" he said.

"I'll kill you, Henry."

There was a moment's silence, complete and still. He stood at the door, the girl lying in his arms waking slowly from sleep, and waited. Each second seemed as though it were an hour long.

"No, you won't do that," he said after a while. "I'm going to beat you to it, Eloise."

Through the thin plaster wall I could hear the smooth slide of his hand into his coat pocket and out again. I could hear the sound of the woman's breath and the gasp in her throat. Through the thin plaster wall I could hear everything that was to happen.

When he pointed the pistol at her, she screamed. He waited until she had cried out, and then he pulled the trigger, not taking careful aim, but nevertheless closing one eye as though he were looking down the sights at her.

The echoes of the explosion drowned out the sound of his running down the hall and the creaking of the floor under his feet.

It was several minutes before the ringing in my ears had died out, and by that time there was the sound of people running through the house from top to bottom, flinging open the doors of the heated rooms and of the unheated rooms as they raced towards us on the second floor.

For a long time I lay against the white plastered wall, trembling because I who was the father had allowed without protest the taking away of the girl, and shaking because I was cold in the unheated room.

The Girl Ellen

The Girl Ellen

ELLEN was nice enough about it. She said she would never have come over to spend the night with Doris if her family had not suddenly left town for the week-end, because she knew Doris and Jim had planned to go swimming that evening. No one could have been more considerate than Ellen.

Finally, she begged them to let her stay at home while they went without her.

It was late in summer, and it had already turned dark. The street lights had just been switched on, but on the porch a dim twilight still lingered.

"Honest, I'd lots rather stay at home," Ellen insisted.

"Forget it," Jim said. "Sometimes it takes three to have a good time, anyway. This might be one of those times."

Under his breath he muttered something. It was the first night in almost a month that he had not had to work, and it would probably be the last time that summer he and Doris could go swimming together. He turned his head from the girl and glared at the street light that twinkled intermittently through the restless, breeze-blown maple leaves.

Jim Gregory did not feel in high spirits anyway. The fellow who worked next to him in the plant had been turned off, and Jim could not help wondering if that were a sign that some of the rest of them would be discharged, too. He had thought about it all the way home, and then he got there and found Ellen with Doris saying that she was afraid to stay by herself while her family was away.

"I'll find something to read," Ellen was saying then, "and I'll have just as good a time right here."

Doris did not have much to say. She liked Ellen a lot, but she was a little sorry it had to happen on just the one night in the month that Jim had off from work.

"I wouldn't think of letting you and Jim take me along," Ellen said for the third or fourth time. "I'd rather stay here."

Jim started to tell her to stay there, but to hush up about it.

"That's different," he said. "If you don't like our company, we probably wouldn't like yours, either."

Ellen jumped off the railing and began tousling Jim's hair. When he found that he could not push her away, he succeeded in catching her hands and pulling her to the arm of the chair. When he got her there, he was sorry he had touched her. He was on the verge of telling her that she was as sticky as molasses.

"Nothing in the world could make me go along with you now," Ellen said. "I wouldn't do anything with a person who talked so mean."

"How do you know I'd like your company?" he said.

She tried to pull away from him. He caught both of her hands in his. Ellen was as yielding as soft rubber in his grip. It surprised him to find her so.

Doris got up and moved towards the door.

"Of course you are going with us," she said with finality. "All three of us are going swimming."

Doris went into the house to get ready, and Ellen got down from the arm of the chair. Her hands slipped through Jim's like silk.

Before he knew what had happened, Ellen had turned around and kissed him lightly on the mouth. The momentary brushing of her lips on his drew him towards her as if to a magnet. When he finally realized what had taken place, she had already turned and had run into the house. He sat upright for a moment, staring after her in a daze. Slowly he sank back into the chair.

When the sound of her had died away in the house, he drew the back of his hand across his lips several times, roughly, until the last trace of her kiss had been wiped away.

While she and Doris were getting ready, he remained on the porch. He had never liked Ellen; she was always running over to see Doris and getting in the way. The longer he thought about it, the more he wished he had worked that night. When he stopped wiping his mouth with the back of his hand, his lips felt bruised, and he was more angry than ever with Ellen for having kissed him.

Doris and Ellen finally came downstairs ready to leave. When the porch light was turned on, he got up and went to the door. Ellen came out first, smiling a little, and Jim could not keep from staring at her again. He felt then, in spite of himself, that he was glad she was going along. Ellen was taller than Doris and, he saw for the first time, prettier. He wondered why he had never noticed that before. He drew the back of his hand over his mouth, quickly, when the touch of her lips came back to him.

When they got to the street where the car was standing, all of them waited indecisively to see who would sit in the middle. Ellen hung back until Doris could decide.

"You sit in the middle," Doris said finally, taking Ellen by the arm and pushing her to the door.

Ellen said nothing, but she hesitated for a moment.

"It's all the same to me," Jim said, trying to appear indifferent.

He made no effort to get into the car until Doris

and Ellen had made up their minds. When Ellen got in, Jim opened the door on his side and sat down beside her. He could not see Doris's face then.

He started the motor, turned around in the street, and drove off faster than usual. It was only nine o'clock and there was plenty of time to reach the swimming pool in the country. However, he was in a hurry to get there.

During the first few minutes of driving, Ellen sat away from him as far as she could, but after they had gone a mile or more, he could feel her close beside him. She was as yielding as he had remembered her being on the porch at home.

After several more minutes he felt that he could not keep from looking at her. Taking his eyes from the road for a moment, he turned and looked at her. Ellen refused to let her eyes meet his. He leaned nearer, hoping to make her look at him.

"You'd better watch where you are going, Jim," Doris said, not turning her head.

He jerked around just in time to keep from running off the road. It made him feel like a fool to have Doris speak like that, but for some reason he did not care. Ellen drew away from him again, and she and Doris began talking together in low tones. After trying for a while, Jim finally stopped trying to overhear what they were saying.

Just before they reached the swimming pool, Jim drew the back of his hand over his mouth several times. His lips still felt bruised where he had mashed them with his knuckles while on the porch at home. But when he closed his eyes, he could still feel, through the numbness and bruise, the brushing of Ellen's lips against his.

"What in the world are you doing, Jim?" Doris cried.

He opened his eyes just in time to jam on the brakes. He turned into the parking lot beside the swimming pool. If Doris had not stopped him, they would have passed it. Jim tried to laugh about it, but he felt like a fool just the same. He wondered what Doris was thinking.

When he stopped the car, Doris jumped out and started for the bath-house without a word. She did not even wait for Ellen.

"I've got to lock up the car, Doris," he said crossly. "Can't you wait a minute?"

Doris stopped and watched him lock the car. When he put the keys into his pocket and started towards her, she turned and walked away. Ellen ran and caught up with her, and they entered the bath-house together.

When Jim got there, they had gone into a locker-room, and he did not see them again.

It did not take him long to change into his bathing suit, and he was in the water ten or fifteen minutes before Doris and Ellen came out of the bath-house. They came together towards him in the pool.

There was so much shouting and splashing of water all around them that Jim could not make them understand what he was trying to say. Giving up, he swam across the pool towards them.

Just before he got to the side of the pool, Doris dived in, plunging out of sight into the ten-foot depth. He and Ellen watched her until she came up. Instead of swimming back to where they were, Doris turned and struck out across the pool to the opposite side. Jim motioned to her with his hands to come back, but Doris did not even shake her head in reply.

"Can't you dive?" he said to Ellen.

"You don't have to snap my head off," she said.

She dived but did not come up for several seconds. Just when he was becoming uneasy, her head appeared thirty feet away, near the center of the pool.

He swam to her.

"You'd better go talk to Doris," Ellen said, backing away from him.

They were both treading water.

"Let's dive off the tower," Jim said.

Ellen shook her head and began swimming towards the shallow end. He followed her.

"Doris won't like it if you don't go over there where she is," Ellen said. "You'd better go, Jim."

He did not look in Doris's direction.

Ellen backed away. Reaching for her hand, Jim caught her and pulled her to him. Even under the water her hands were as yielding as they had been on the porch at home. More than ever he felt that she was like soft rubber in his hands.

"You shouldn't do that," she said. "Jim, I——"

Somebody splashed water near by, and a wave broke over their heads. Ellen came up choking. Quickly grasping her around the waist, Jim lifted her so no more water could reach her head. She was all right after a moment, but he did not release her. Once he had her in his arms, he felt he could never turn her loose again. It was like holding a wild rabbit in his arms, knowing the frightened, panting animal would make a break for freedom at the slightest chance. He squeezed her all the more tightly.

"Don't do that, Jim," she said.

She strained to break away from him, but Jim's arms were like iron bands around her. Once, for a moment, she relaxed in his arms. He crushed her more tightly than ever.

"Jim," she said, "Jim, we can't . . ."

Out of the corner of his eye he saw Doris jump to her feet from the bench where she had been sitting and walk to the edge of the pool. He did not look long enough to see whether she had dived in or whether she went back to the bench.

"Please don't hold me any more," Ellen said. "Let's go with Doris. I can't let you hold me like this."

"She's all right," Jim heard himself say. "Don't worry about her."

"But you've got to stop, Jim. Please don't hold me any more. I'm going with Doris."

He pulled her with him to the other side of the pool, ignoring every word she said. When they got to the rim, Ellen broke away from him and dived under the water. He plunged after her.

When he came up, he could see neither Ellen nor Doris. For a while he thought they were ducking out of sight, and he went under again himself, swimming along the side of the pool with his eyes open in the water. He could see neither of them.

After thirty or forty seconds under the water he came up for breath. He came up just in time to see Ellen climbing the ladder out of the water. He splashed after her.

"Where's Doris?" Ellen asked him.

He climbed out and stood beside her, looking around the pool. Doris was not to be seen among the fifteen or twenty persons in the water.

"Maybe she's gone into the bath-house," he said.

Ellen's fingers caught his, closing over his hand.

"No," she said, trembling all over. "No, she didn't go into the bath-house. She couldn't have, because I've been watching all the time."

Jim walked hurriedly around the pool, searching each face in the crowd. When he got back, he sat down on a bench. Ellen dropped beside him.

"Where is she, Jim?" Ellen said.

"She's all right," he said. "She'll show up in a minute."

"But she wouldn't go off like this, Jim."

Jim laughed.

"Maybe she didn't like it because I was in the water with you so long," he said. "She'll be back as soon as she gets over it."

Ellen drew away from him, moving to the other end of the bench.

"I shouldn't have let you," she said, covering her face with her hands. "I didn't know what I was doing. It was my fault. I should have known better."

He got up and left her to go to the refreshment stand. He brought back two cones of ice cream and sat down on the bench.

"I wouldn't have hurt Doris for anything in the world," Ellen said, covering her face.

"You didn't hurt her," Jim insisted. "She just went into the bath-house."

Ellen tried to eat the ice cream, but she could not swallow it. She handed the cone back to Jim and ran into the bath-house. She was back in less than a minute.

"Doris isn't in the locker-room, Jim, but her clothes are!" she cried.

Jim ran to the pool and tried to see down into the bottom of it. The people all around him were diving and splashing in the water.

He began to tremble.

"Jim!" Ellen cried. "'Something has happened to Doris!"

"How could anything happen to her. She can swim as good as I can. What makes you think something happened?"

Ellen screamed.

The guard who had been sitting in a chair reading a magazine jumped to his feet and ran towards them.

"What's the matter with you people?" he said.

"A girl is missing!" Ellen cried excitedly. "Doris isn't here. I haven't seen her for nearly half an hour."

The guard ran to the drain tap and opened the outlet. The water began to sink immediately.

By that time a dozen or more persons had begun diving and searching in the ten-foot depth. Jim and Ellen stood on the edge, leaning over as far as they could, watching.

When the water had drained to the four-foot mark,

somebody said something. He went under the water and came up slowly. Jim jumped into the pool and felt under the water with his hands. Together they brought up the body of a girl. It was Doris.

When she had been carried out of the pool and stretched on the ground, Ellen began crying. The guard had already begun working over Doris, and somebody had thought to call an ambulance.

Doris's rubber bathing cap had slipped off her head, and her long brown hair was tangled around her. Jim jumped into the water and began searching frantically for the rubber cap while the guard worked over Doris. Jim could think of nothing else to do.

In spite of the guard's determined attempt to resuscitate her, Doris was already dead when they lifted her on the stretcher and placed her in the ambulance.

Jim slumped down in a corner of the bath-house. No one saw him there, and long after everybody else had hurriedly dressed and left, he was still there. The lights had been turned off when he opened his eyes.

Feeling his way outside, he did not think of changing into his clothes. He walked outside into the parking lot where his car was standing. When he remembered that his keys were in his clothes inside the bath-house, he started walking towards town without another thought. If the keys had been anyplace else, he would have gone for them; but he could not turn his face again in the direction of the swimming pool.

He finally got home, but he could not remember how he had managed to find his way when he could recall nothing that had taken place since leaving the parking lot. The hall light was burning as they had left it, and he found an unlocked window through which he managed to climb inside.

Stumbling through the house from room to room, he at last fell on his hands and knees on the floor, and a moment later he felt himself fall over on his side. The last thing he remembered doing was wondering if Ellen would be there when he woke up.

The Growing Season

The Growing Season

THE heat was enough to drive anybody crazy. The wire-grass was growing faster than Jesse English could keep it chopped down and covered up. He had been going over the twelve acres of cotton for five days already, and he was just about ready to give up.

At noon when his wife called him to dinner, Jesse unhitched the mule from the scraper and turned him loose. The mule walked unsteadily towards the barn, stumbling over the rows as if he had blind-staggers. Jesse's eyes were bloodshot by the heat, and he was afraid he was going to get a sunstroke. He got to the house, but he could not eat anything. He stretched out on the porch, his straw hat over his face to shut out the glare of the sun, feeling as if he could never get up again as long as he lived.

Lizzie came to the door and told him to get up and eat the meal she had cooked. Jesse did not answer her, and after a while she went back inside out of sight.

The rattling of the trace chain in the yard woke Jesse up. He raised himself on his elbow and looked out under the chinaberry tree at Fiddler. Fiddler crawled around the tree, winding the chain around the trunk of the chinaberry. When Fiddler had wound the chain as far as he could, he lay down again.

Jesse stared at Fiddler with his bloodshot eyes burning into his head until he could not stand it any longer. He dug his knuckles into his eye sockets until the pain had left for a while.

Fiddler got up and made as if to stand. Instead, he pitched forward like a drunken man, falling into a mass. Jesse felt a new rush of blood in his head each time Fiddler rattled the chain. While watching him, he began to wonder what was going to happen to his crop of cotton.

It had rained for a solid week just when the cotton was ready to hoe, and before he could catch up with it, the wire-grass had got ahead of him. Lizzie had had a sunstroke the year before, and every time she stayed in the sun fifteen or twenty minutes she fainted. She could not help him hoe; there was nobody to help him. There was not even a Negro on the place.

When he looked out over the field, he realized how little he had accomplished since sun-up that morning. He did not see how he would ever be able to clear out the grass before the cotton plants got choked out.

The trace chain rattled again. Jesse pushed himself on his hands and feet to the edge of the porch and sat there staring at Fiddler. Lizzie came to the door once more and told him to come and eat his dinner, but he did not hear her.

Fiddler turned over on the ground and lay with his head up against the trunk of the chinaberry tree.

Sitting on the edge of the porch with his feet swinging back and forth, Jesse rubbed his eyes with his knuckles and tried to reason clearly. The heat, even in the shade of the porch roof, was blinding him. His eyes burned like hot chestnuts in his head. When he heard Fiddler rattle the chain again, he tried to stare at him through the heat, but Fiddler was by then no more than a blue patch in the yard.

The crop was going to ruin because there was nobody to help him get the grass out before the cotton plants were choked to death by the wire-grass.

Jesse eased himself off the edge of the porch and climbed the steps and went into the hall. His shotgun was standing in the corner behind the door. It was kept loaded all the time, and he did not stop to see if there were any shells in the barrels.

"Your dinner's getting spoiled, Jesse," his wife said somewhere in the house.

He did not answer her.

Outside in the sun and heat once more, Jesse could see the wire-grass choking the life out of his crop of cotton. He ran to the far end of the yard and out into the field and began kicking the cotton plants and grass with his feet. Even then the wire-grass sprang back like coils in a bedspring. The cotton plants he had kicked from their roots began slowly to wilt in the noonday heat. By the time he had turned away, the plants had shriveled up and died.

He went back into the yard and kicked the trace chain. One end was fastened to the chinaberry tree, and the other end was clamped around Fiddler's neck. He stood the shotgun against the tree and began fumbling with the clamp. While he was stooped over, Lizzie came to the porch again.

"What are you aiming to do with that shotgun, Jesse?" she asked, shading her eyes with her hands.

When he did not answer her, she ran down the steps and raced across the yard to the chinaberry.

The clamp was unfastened then. Jesse grabbed the gun and jerked the chain. He jerked the chain harder the next time, and Fiddler rolled to his feet and went wobbling across the yard like a drunken man trying to walk.

Lizzie tried to jerk the chain out of Jesse's hand. He pushed her aside.

"Jesse!" she screamed at him. "Jesse, what you going to do with Fiddler!"

He pushed her behind him. Fiddler wobbled on his undeveloped legs and Jesse poked him upright with the gun-stock each time he looked as if he would fall.

Lizzie came screaming after them and fell around her husband's legs. Jesse got away from her before she could lock her arms around his knees.

Fiddler had started running towards the barn. Jesse ran behind, holding the gun ahead so he could prod Fiddler in the direction he wanted him to go.

The crop was ruined. But he had forgotten all about the wire-grass choking out the tender cotton plants. The grass had got ahead of him before he could stop it. If Lizzie had not been sunstruck, or if he had had anybody else to help him, he could have saved his cotton. The wire-grass on twelve acres was too much for one man, once he fell behind.

His eyes were so bloodshot he could not see Fiddler very well. The heat and the throbbing in his head made him forget everything except that he had to get Fiddler out behind the barn where the gully was. He threw a corncob at the mule to get him out of Fiddler's way. The mule went into the barn.

Fiddler ran off in another direction, but Jesse headed him back to the gully with the butt end of the shotgun. He hit Fiddler again with the stock to keep him from going in the wrong direction.

Lizzie was screaming in the front yard. She did not have her sunbonnet on, and she had already got a touch of heat.

When they got to the gully, Jesse shoved Fiddler

down into it. Fiddler lay on the bottom of the wash, digging at the sides and trying to get out.

Jesse raised his gun to sight down the barrels, and all he could see was a wiggling gray mass against the red clay gully-bank. He pulled the trigger anyway, and waited a moment. Without lowering the gun, he fired the second shell at Fiddler.

Fiddler was making more noise than he had ever made before. Jesse sat down on the side of the gully and rubbed his eyes with his knuckles. He felt the dried earth give way under his knees, and he moved back a little to keep from sliding down into the gully where Fiddler was floundering like a fish that had been tossed upon dry land.

"Stop that kicking and squealing, and die, damn you!" Jesse shouted. "Die! Damn you, die!"

He could not sit there any longer. He had waited as long as he could wait for Fiddler to stop thrashing around in the gully. The birdshot in the shells was strong enough to kill a mule at short range, but they had not been strong enough to kill Fiddler.

Lizzie screaming under the chinaberry tree and the heat and the blazing sun overhead sent Jesse running to the woodpile at the back of the house. He grabbed up the ax and came running back to the gully. Fiddler was still thrashing around on the bottom like a chicken with its head cut off. Jesse jumped down the bank and struck at Fiddler three or four times. When he stopped, blood was all over the ax-handle and blade, and the bottoms of his overall legs were soaked with it.

After a while Fiddler lay still, and Jesse walked down to the lower end of the gully where the banks were not so steep and climbed to the top. On the way back to the house he could see Lizzie lying on the ground under the chinaberry tree where Fiddler had been kept chained.

He carried the ax to the woodpile and swung the blade into a hickory log. After that he sat down on the woodpile and wiped his face with his hands and tried to stop the burning of his eyeballs by digging at them with his knuckles.

From somewhere a breeze came up, and the wind against his hot face made him feel better all over. He ran his thumb under one overall strap and threw it off. The breeze blowing against his wet shirt and skin felt like a gentle rain.

One of the hounds that had been sleeping under the house got up and walked out to the woodpile and began licking the ax-handle. Jesse watched him until he had finished. When the dog started licking his overall legs, Jesse kicked him with all his might. The hound tumbled to his feet and ran yelping back under the house.

Jesse wiped his face with his hands again, and got

up. He found the hoe leaning against the side of the house. He carried it to the porch and pulled the rat-tailed file out of the weatherboarding where it had been stuck since the last time he used it.

He thought he heard his wife stumbling through the hall of the house.

Propping the hoe against the porch, Jesse began filing the blade until it was as keen as a corn-knife. After that was done, he jabbed the file back into the weatherboarding and walked towards the cotton field, bareheaded in the hot sun, carrying the hoe over his shoulder.

Jesse was not certain, but he felt he might be able to save his crop. The wire-grass could not stand up under a sharp hoe-blade, and he could go back and file his hoe with the rat-tailed file whenever it wanted sharpening.

Daughter

Daughter

At sunrise a Negro on his way to the big house to feed the mules had taken the word to Colonel Henry Maxwell, and Colonel Henry phoned the sheriff. The sheriff had hustled Jim into town and locked him up in the jail, and then he went home and ate breakfast.

Jim walked around the empty cellroom while he was buttoning his shirt, and after that he sat down on the bunk and tied his shoelaces. Everything that morning had taken place so quickly that he had not even had time to get a drink of water. He got up and went to the water bucket near the door, but the sheriff had forgotten to put water in it.

By that time there were several men standing in the jailyard. Jim went to the window and looked out when he heard them talking. Just then another automobile drove up, and six or seven men got out. Other men were coming towards the jail from both directions of the street.

"What was the trouble out at your place this morning, Jim?" somebody said.

Jim stuck his chin between the bars and looked at

the faces in the crowd. He knew everyone there.

While he was trying to figure out how everybody in town had heard about his being there, somebody else spoke to him.

"It must have been an accident, wasn't it, Jim?"

A colored boy hauling a load of cotton to the gin drove up the street. When the wagon got in front of the jail, the boy whipped up the mules with the ends of the reins and made them trot.

"I hate to see the State have a grudge against you, Jim," somebody said.

The sheriff came down the street swinging a tin dinner-pail in his hand. He pushed through the crowd, unlocked the door, and set the pail inside.

Several men came up behind the sheriff and looked over his shoulder into the jail.

"Here's your breakfast my wife fixed up for you, Jim. You'd better eat a little, Jim boy."

Jim looked at the pail, at the sheriff, at the open jail door, and he shook his head.

"I don't feel hungry," he said. "Daughter's been hungry, though—awful hungry."

The sheriff backed out the door, his hand going to the handle of his pistol. He backed out so quickly that he stepped on the toes of the men behind him.

"Now, don't you get careless, Jim boy," he said. "Just sit and calm yourself."

He shut the door and locked it. After he had gone a few steps towards the street, he stopped and looked into the chamber of his pistol to make sure it had been loaded.

The crowd outside the window pressed in closer. Some of the men rapped on the bars until Jim came and looked out. When he saw them, he stuck his chin between the iron and gripped his hands around it.

"How come it to happen, Jim?" somebody asked. "It must have been an accident, wasn't it?"

Jim's long thin face looked as if it would come through the bars. The sheriff came up to the window to see if everything was all right.

"Now, just take it easy, Jim boy," he said.

The man who had asked Jim to tell what had happened, elbowed the sheriff out of the way. The other men crowded closer.

"How come, Jim?" the man said. "Was it an accident?"

"No," Jim said, his fingers twisting about the bars. "I picked up my shotgun and done it."

The sheriff pushed towards the window again.

"Go on, Jim, and tell us what it's all about."

Jim's face squeezed between the bars until it looked as though only his ears kept his head from coming through.

"Daughter said she was hungry, and I just couldn't

stand it no longer. I just couldn't stand to hear her say it."

"Don't get all excited now, Jim boy," the sheriff said, pushing forward one moment and being elbowed away the next.

"She waked up in the middle of the night again and said she was hungry. I just couldn't stand to hear her say it."

Somebody pushed all the way through the crowd until he got to the window.

"Why, Jim, you could have come and asked me for something for her to eat, and you know I'd have given you all I got in the world."

The sheriff pushed forward once more.

"That wasn't the right thing to do," Jim said. "I've been working all year and I made enough for all of us to eat."

He stopped and looked down into the faces on the other side of the bars.

"I made enough working on shares, but they came and took it all away from me. I couldn't go around begging after I'd made enough to keep us. They just came and took it all off. Then Daughter woke up again this morning saying she was hungry, and I just couldn't stand it no longer."

"You'd better go and get on the bunk now, Jim boy," the sheriff said.

"It don't seem right that the little girl ought to be shot like that," somebody said.

"Daughter said she was hungry," Jim said. "She'd been saying that for all of the past month. Daughter'd wake up in the middle of the night and say it. I just couldn't stand it no longer."

"You ought to have sent her over to my house, Jim. Me and my wife could have fed her something, somehow. It don't look right to kill a little girl like her."

"I'd made enough for all of us," Jim said. "I just couldn't stand it no longer. Daughter'd been hungry all the past month."

"Take it easy, Jim boy," the sheriff said, trying to push forward.

The crowd swayed from side to side.

"And so you just picked up the gun this morning and shot her?" somebody asked.

"When she woke up this morning saying she was hungry, I just couldn't stand it."

The crowd pushed closer. Men were coming towards the jail from all directions, and those who were then arriving pushed forward to hear what Jim had to say.

"The State has got a grudge against you now, Jim," somebody said, "but somehow it don't seem right."

"I can't help it," Jim said. "Daughter woke up again this morning that way."

The jailyard, the street, and the vacant lot on the other side were filled with men and boys. All of them were pushing forward to hear Jim. Word had spread all over town by that time that Jim Carlisle had shot and killed his eight-year-old daughter, Clara.

"Who does Jim share-crop for?" somebody asked.

"Colonel Henry Maxwell," a man in the crowd said. "Colonel Henry has had Jim out there about nine or ten years."

"Henry Maxwell didn't have no business coming and taking all the shares. He's got plenty of his own. It aint right for Henry Maxwell to come and take Jim's, too."

The sheriff was pushing forward once more.

"The State's got a grudge against Jim now," somebody said. "Somehow it don't seem right, though."

The sheriff pushed his shoulder into the crowd of men and worked his way in closer.

A man shoved the sheriff away.

"Why did Henry Maxwell come and take your share of the crop, Jim?"

"He said I owed it to him because one of his mules died about a month ago."

The sheriff got in front of the barred window.

"You ought to go to the bunk now and rest some, Jim boy," he said. "Take off your shoes and stretch out, Jim boy."

He was elbowed out of the way.

"You didn't kill the mule, did you, Jim?"

"The mule dropped dead in the barn," Jim said. "I wasn't nowhere around. It just dropped dead."

The crowd was pushing harder. The men in front were jammed against the jail, and the men behind were trying to get within earshot. Those in the middle were squeezed against each other so tightly they could not move in any direction. Everyone was talking louder.

Jim's face pressed between the bars and his fingers gripped the iron until the knuckles were white.

The milling crowd was moving across the street to the vacant lot. Somebody was shouting. He climbed up on an automobile and began swearing at the top of his lungs.

A man in the middle of the crowd pushed his way out and went to his automobile. He got in and drove off alone.

Jim stood holding to the bars and looking through the window. The sheriff had his back to the crowd, and he was saying something to Jim. Jim did not hear what he said.

A man on his way to the gin with a load of cotton stopped to find out what the trouble was. He looked at the crowd in the vacant lot for a moment, and then he turned around and looked at Jim behind the bars.

The shouting across the street was growing louder.

"What's the trouble, Jim?"

Somebody on the other side of the street came to the wagon. He put his foot on a spoke in the wagon wheel and looked up at the man on the cotton while he talked.

"Daughter woke up this morning again saying she was hungry," Jim said.

The sheriff was the only person who heard him.

The man on the load of cotton jumped to the ground, tied the reins to the wagon wheel, and pushed through the crowd to the car where all the shouting and swearing was being done. After listening for a while, he came back to the street, called a Negro who was standing with several other Negroes on the corner, and handed him the reins. The Negro drove off with the cotton towards the gin, and the man went back into the crowd.

Just then the man who had driven off alone in his car came back. He sat for a moment behind the steering wheel, and then he jumped to the ground. He opened the rear door and took out a crowbar that was as long as he was tall.

"Pry that jail door open and let Jim out," somebody said. "It aint right for him to be in there."

The crowd in the vacant lot was moving again.

The man who had been standing on top of the automobile jumped to the ground, and the men moved towards the street in the direction of the jail.

The first man to reach it jerked the six-foot crowbar out of the soft earth where it had been jabbed.

The sheriff backed off.

"Now, take it easy, Jim boy," he said.

He turned and started walking rapidly up the street towards his house.

Blue Boy

Blue Boy

TWO HOURS after dinner they were still sitting in the air-tight overheated parlor. A dull haze of tobacco smoke was packed in layers from the table-top to the ceiling, and around the chairs hovered the smell of dried perspiration, intestinal belches, and stale perfume. The New Year's Day turkey-and-hog dinner had made the women droopy and dull-eyed; the men were stretched out in their chairs with their legs spread out and their heads thrown back, looking as if around each swollen belly a hundred feet of stuffed sausage-casing had been wound.

Grady Walters sat up, rubbed his red-veined face, and looked at his guests. After a while he went to the door and called for one of his Negro servants. He sent the Negro on the run for Blue Boy.

After he had closed the door tightly, Grady walked back towards his chair, looking at the drowsy men and women through the haze of blue tobacco smoke and stale perfume. It had been more than an hour since anyone had felt like saying anything.

"What time of day is it getting to be, Grady?" Rob Howard asked, rubbing first his eyes and then his belly.

"Time to have a little fun," Grady said.

Blue Boy came through the back door and shuffled down the hall to the parlor where the people were. He dragged his feet sideways over the floor, making a sound like soy beans being poured into a wooden barrel.

"We been waiting here all afternoon for you to come in here and show the folks some fun, Blue Boy," Grady said. "All my visitors are just itching to laugh. Reckon you can make them shake their sides, Blue Boy?"

Blue Boy grinned at the roomful of men and women. He dug his hands into his overall pockets and made some kind of unintelligible sound in his throat.

Rob Howard asked Grady what Blue Boy could do. Several of the women sat up and began rubbing powder into the pores of their skin.

The colored boy grinned some more, stretching his neck in a semicircle.

"Blue Boy," Grady said, "show these white-folks how you caught that shoat the other day and bit him to death. Go on, Blue Boy! Let's see how you chewed that shoat to death with your teeth."

For several moments the boy's lips moved like eyelids a-flutter, and he made a dash for the door. Grady caught him by the shoulder and tossed him back into the center of the room.

"All right, Blue Boy," Grady shouted at him. "Do what I told you to do. Show the white-folks how you bit that pig to death."

Blue Boy made deeper sounds in his throat. What he said sounded more unintelligible than Gullah. Nobody but Grady could understand what he was trying to say.

"It don't make no difference if you aint got a shoat here to kill," Grady answered him. "Go on and show the white-folks how you killed one the other day for me."

Blue Boy dropped on his hands and knees, making sounds as if he were trying to protest. Grady nudged him with his foot, prodding him on.

The Negro boy suddenly began to snarl and bite, acting as if he himself had been turned into a snarling, biting shoat. He grabbed into the air, throwing his arms around an imaginary young hog, and began to tear its throat with his sharp white teeth. The Howards and Hannafords crowded closer, trying to see the semi-idiot go through the actions of a bloodthirsty maniac.

Down on the floor, Blue Boy's face was contorted and swollen. His eyes glistened, and his mouth drooled. He was doing all he could to please Grady Walters.

When he had finished, the Howards and Hannafords fell back, fanning their faces and wiping the backs of their hands with their handkerchiefs. Even Grady fanned his flushed face when Blue Boy stopped and rolled over on the floor exhausted.

"What else can he do, Grady?" the youngest of the Hannaford women asked.

"Anything I tell him to do," Grady said. "I've got Blue Boy trained. He does whatever I tell him."

They looked down at the small, thin, blue-skinned, seventeen-year-old Negro on the floor. His clothes were ragged, and his thick kinky hair was almost as long as a Negro woman's. He looked the same, except in size, as he did the day, twelve years before, when Grady brought him to the big house from one of the share-croppers' cabins. Blue Boy had never become violent, and he obeyed every word of Grady's. Grady had taught him to do tricks as he would instruct a young puppy to roll over on his back when bidden. Blue Boy always obeyed, but sometimes he was not quick enough to suit Grady, and then Grady flew into him with the leather belly-band that hung on a nail on the back porch.

The Howards and Hannafords had sat down again, but the Negro boy still lay on the floor. Grady had not told him to get up.

"What's wrong with him, Grady?" Rob Howard asked.

"He aint got a grain of sense," Grady said, laughing

a little. "See how he grins all the time? A calf is born with more sense than he's got right now."

"Why don't you send him to the insane asylum, then?"

"What for?" Grady said. "He's more fun than a barrel of monkeys. I figure he's worth keeping just for the hell of it. If I sent him off to the asylum, I'd miss my good times with him. I wouldn't take a hundred dollars for Blue Boy."

"What else can he do?" Henry Hannaford asked.

"I'll show you," Grady said. "Here, Blue Boy, get up and do that monkey-shine dance for the white-folks. Show them what you can do with your feet."

Blue Boy got up, pushing himself erect with hands and feet. He stood grinning for a while at the men and women in a circle around him.

"Go on, Blue Boy, shake your feet for the white-folks," Grady told him, pointing at Blue Boy's feet. "Do the monkey-shine, Blue Boy."

The boy began to shuffle his shoes on the floor, barely raising them off the surface. Grady started tapping his feet, moving them faster and faster all the time. Blue Boy watched him, and after a while his own feet began going faster. He kept it up until he was dancing so fast his breath began to give out. His eyes were swelling, and it looked as if his balls would pop out of his head any moment. The arteries in his neck got larger and rounder.

"That nigger can do the monkey-shine better than any nigger I ever saw," Henry Hannaford said.

Blue Boy sank into a heap on the floor, the arteries in his neck pumping and swelling until some of the women in the room covered their faces to keep from seeing them.

It did not take Blue Boy long to get his wind back, but he still lay on the floor. Grady watched him until he thought he had recovered enough to stand up again.

"What else can your trained nigger do, Grady?" Rob Howard asked. "Looks like you would have learned him a heap of tricks in ten or twelve years' time."

"If it wasn't getting so late in the day, I'd tell him to do all he knows," Grady said. "I'll let him do one more, anyway."

Blue Boy had not moved from the floor.

"Get up, Blue Boy," Grady said. "Get up and stand up on your feet."

Blue Boy got up grinning. His head turned once more on his rubbery neck, stretching in a semicircle around the room. He grinned at the white faces about him.

"Take out that blacksnake and whip it to a frazzle,"

Grady told him. "Take it out, Blue Boy, and show the white-folks what you can do."

Blue Boy grinned, stretching his rubbery neck until it looked as if it would come loose from his body.

"What's he going to do now, Grady?" Rob Howard asked.

"You just wait and see, Rob," Grady said. "All right, Blue Boy, do like I said. Whip that blacksnake."

The youngest Hannaford woman giggled. Blue Boy turned and stared at her with his round white eyeballs. He grinned until Grady prodded him on.

"Now I reckon you folks know why I didn't send him off to the insane asylum," Grady said. "I have a heap more fun out of Blue Boy than I would with anything else you can think of. He can't hoe cotton, or pick it, and he hasn't even got enough sense to chop a piece of stovewood, but he makes up for all that by learning to do the tricks I teach him."

Once more Blue Boy's eyes began to pop in the sockets of his skull, and the arteries in his neck began to pump and swell. He dropped to his knees and his once rubbery neck was as rigid as a table-leg. The grinning lines on his face had congealed into welt-like scars.

The Howards and Hannafords, who had come from five counties to eat Grady's New Year's Day turkey-and-hog dinner, gulped and wheezed at the sight of

Blue Boy. He was beginning to droop like a wilting stalk of pig-weed. Then he fell from his knees.

With his face pressed against the splintery floor, the grooves in his cheeks began to soften, and his grinning features glistened in the drying perspiration. His breathing became inaudible, and the swollen arteries in his neck were as rigid as taut-drawn ropes.

Slow Death

Slow Death

ALL DAY we had been sitting in the piano box waiting for the rain to stop. Below us, twenty feet away, the muddy Savannah River oozed past, carrying to the sea the dead pines and rotted mule collars of the uplands.

Overhead, the newly completed Fifth Street Bridge kept us dry. We had stacked piles of brickbats under the corners of the piano box to keep the floor of it dry, and the water that drained from the bridge and red-clay embankment passed under us on its way to the swollen river.

Every once in a while Dave got up on his hands and knees and turned the straw over. It was banana straw, and it was soggy and foul-smelling. There was just enough room for the two of us in the crate, and if the straw was not evenly strewn, it made lumps under our backs and sides that felt as hard as bricks.

Just behind us was a family of four living in a cluster of dry-goods boxes. The boxes had been joined together by means of holes cut in the sides, like those of doghouses, and the mass of packing cases provided four or five rooms. The woman had two dominique hens. These she kept in the box with her all the time, day and night, stroking their feathers so they would be persuaded to lay eggs for her. There were a dozen or more other crates under the South Carolina side of the bridge; when old men and women, starved and yellow, died in one of them, their bodies were carried down to the river and lowered into the muddy water; when babies were born, people leaned over the railings above and listened to the screams of birth and threw peanut shells over the side.

At dark the rain stopped. The sky looked as if it would not clear before morning, and we knew it would drizzle all night. Dave was restless, and he could not stay in the box any longer.

"Come on, Mike," he said. "Let's get out of here and dig up something to eat somewhere."

I followed him through the red mud up the side of the embankment to the pavement above. We walked through puddles of water, washing the sticky red clay from our feet as we went.

Dave had fifty cents in his pocket and I was determined not to let him buy me anything to eat. He had baled waste paper in a basement factory off and on for two weeks, and when he worked, he made fifty cents a day. He had worked the day before in the basement, and the money had been kept all that time.

When we crossed the river into Georgia, I turned sharply to the right and started running up the levee away from Dave. I had gone fifty yards when he caught me by the sweater and made me stop. Then he took the fist out of his pocket and showed me the fifty-cent piece.

"Don't worry about me, Dave," I told him, catching his wrist and forcing his hand back into his pocket. "I'll get by till tomorrow. I've got the promise of a half-day job, and that ought to be good for a dollar —a half, anyway. Go on and buy yourself a good meal, Dave."

"No," Dave said, jerking the fist out of his pants. "We'll split it."

He pulled me along with him towards the city. We broke through the levee grass and went down the embankment to the pavement. There was a dull orange glow in the low sky ahead of us, and the traffic in the streets sounded like an angry mob fighting for their lives.

We walked along together, splashing through the shallow puddles of rainwater on the pavement, going towards the city. Suddenly Dave stopped squarely in the middle of a sheet of rainwater that had not drained off into the sewers.

"You're young, Mike," he said, catching my sweater and shaking it as a dog does a pillow. "I'm old, but you're young. You can find out what to do, and come back and tell me, and we'll do it."

"What's the matter, Dave?" I asked him. "What are you talking about?"

He waved his arm in an arc that took in most of the world.

"Somewhere there's people who know what to do about being down and out. If you could find out from them, and come back, we could do it."

"It'll take more than two of us, Dave. We'll have to get a lot more on our side first."

"Don't worry about that," he said. "As soon as the people know what to do, and how to do it, we can go up and run hell out of those fat bastards who won't give us our jobs back."

"Maybe it's not time yet, Dave."

"Not time yet! Haven't I been out of my job two years now? How much time do you want? Now's the time, before all of us starve to death and get carried feet first down into that mud-slough of a river."

Before I could say anything, he had turned around and started up the street again. I ran and caught up with him. We splashed through the puddles, dodging the deepest-looking ones.

Dave had had a good job in a fertilizer plant in South Augusta two years before. But they turned him out one day, and they would not take him back. There were seventy men in the crowd that was laid off that time. Dave would never tell me what had happened to the rest of them, but I knew what had happened to Dave. After he had run behind in house rent for six or seven months, the landlord told him to move out. Dave would not do it. He said he was going to stay there until he got back his job in the fertilizer plant in South Augusta. Dave stayed.

Dave stayed in the house for another four months, but long before the end of that time the window-sashes and doors of the building had been taken out and carried off by the owner. When winter came, the rain soaked the house until it was as soggy as a log of punkwood. After that, the cold winds of January drove through the dwelling, whistling through the wide slits of the house like a madman breathing through clenched teeth. There was no wood or coal to burn in the fireplaces. There were only two quilts and a blanket for Dave and his wife and three children. Two of the children died before the end of January. In February his wife went. In March there was a special prayer service in one of the churches for Dave and his eleven-year-old daughter, but Dave said all he got out of it was a pair of khaki pants with two holes the size of dinner plates in the seat.

Dave did not know whether his remaining daughter had died, or whether she was being taken care of by charity, or whether she had been taken in to live at a whorehouse. The last time he had seen her was when a policeman came and took her away one morning, leaving Dave sitting in a corner of the windowless house wrapped in the two quilts and a blanket.

We had reached Seventh Street by that time. The Plaza was hidden in fog, and all around it the tall hotels and government buildings rose like century-old tombstones damp and gray.

"Go on and eat, Dave," I told him again. "When you get through, I'll meet you here, and we'll walk back to the river and get in out of the cold."

"I'm not going a step till you come with me."

"But I'm not hungry, Dave. I wouldn't lie to you. I'm not hungry."

"I'm not going to eat, then," he said again.

The night was getting colder and more raw all the time. Some drain water in the gutter at our feet lay in a long snake-like stream, and it looked as if it would freeze before much longer. The wind was coming up, blowing the fog down the river and stinging our backs. A moment later it had shifted its course and was stinging our faces.

"Hurry up, Dave," I begged him. "There's no sense in our standing here and freezing. I'll meet you in half an hour."

Dave caught my sweater and pulled me back. The

roar of speeding automobiles and the crashing rumble of motor trucks made such a din in the street that we had to shout to make ourselves heard.

Just as I was about to try again to make him get something to eat for himself, I turned around and saw a black sedan coming around the corner behind us. It was coming fast, more than forty miles an hour, and it was on the inside, cutting the corner.

I pulled at Dave to get him out of the way, because his back was turned to the sedan and he could not see it.

He evidently thought I was trying to make him go to the restaurant alone, because he pulled away from me and stepped backward out of my reach. It was too late then to try to grab him and get him out of the way, and all I could do was to shout at him as loud as I could above the roar in the street. Dave must still have thought I was trying to make him go to the restaurant alone, because he stepped backward again. As he stepped backward the second time, the bumper and right front mudguard on the sedan struck him. He was knocked to the sidewalk like a duck-pin.

The man who was driving the big sedan had cut the corner by at least three feet, because the wheels had jumped the curb.

There was a queer-looking expression on Dave's face.

The driver stopped, and he walked back to where we were. By that time people had begun to gather from all directions, and we were surrounded on all sides.

"Are you hurt, Dave?" I asked him, getting down on the sidewalk with him.

The driver had pushed through the crowd, and when I looked up, he was standing at Dave's feet looking down at us, scowling.

"Mike," Dave said, turning his face towards me, "Mike, the half-dollar piece is in my right-hand pants pocket."

His fingers were clutching my hand, and he held me tight, as though he were afraid he would fall.

"Forget the half, Dave," I begged him. "Tell me if you're hurt. If you are, I'll get a doctor right away."

Dave opened his eyes, looking straight up at me. His shoulders moved slightly, and he held me tighter.

"There's nothing wrong with him," the driver of the sedan said, pushing the crowd away from him with his elbows. "There's nothing the matter with him. He's faking."

The man stood erect above us, looking down at Dave. His mouth was partly open, and his lips were rounded, appearing to be swollen. When he spoke, there was no motion on his lips; they looked like a bloodless growth on his mouth, curling outward.

"Mike," Dave said, "I guess I'll have to give up trying to get my job back. It's too late now; I won't have time enough."

The man above us was talking to several persons in the crowd. His lips seemed to be too stiff to move when he spoke; they looked by that time like rolls of unbaked dough.

"He's faking," he said again. "He thinks he can get some money out of me, but I'm wise to the tricks of these bums. There's nothing wrong with him. He's no more hurt than I am."

I could hear people all around us talking. There was one fellow in the crowd behind me talking loud enough for everyone to hear. I could not see his face, but no one could have failed to hear every word he said.

"Sure, he's a bum. That's why they don't take him to the hospital. What in hell do they care about a bum? They wouldn't give him a ride to the hospital, because it might cost them something. They might get the goddam sedan bloody. They don't want bum's blood on the goddam pretty upholstery."

I unbuttoned Dave's sweater and put my hand under his shirt, trying to find out if there were any bones broken in his shoulder. Dave had closed his eyes again, but his fingers were still gripped tightly around my wrist.

"He's faking," the driver said. "These bums try all kinds of tricks to get money. There's nothing wrong with him. He's not hurt. He's faking."

The fellow behind us in the crowd was talking again.

"Why don't you take him to the hospital in your sedan, Dough-Face?"

The man looked the crowd over, but he made no reply.

I drew my hand out from under Dave's shirt and saw blood on my fingers. It had not come from his shoulder. It came from the left side of his chest where he had struck the pavement when the sedan knocked him down and rolled over him. I put my hand inside again, feeling for broken bones. Dave's body on that side was soft and wet, and I had felt his heart beating as though I had held it in the palm of my hand.

"How about taking him to the hospital?" I said to the driver looking down at us. "He's been hurt."

"That's the way these bums fake," the driver said, looking from face to face in the crowd. "There's nothing wrong with him. He's not hurt. If he was hurt, he'd yell about it. You don't hear him yelling and groaning, do you? He's just lying there waiting for me to throw him a ten or a twenty. If I did that and drove off, he'd jump up and beat it around the block before I could get out of sight. I know these bums; all they want is money. That one down there is faking just like all the rest of them do. He's no more hurt than I am."

I tried to get up and lift Dave in my arms. We could carry him to the hospital, even if the driver wouldn't take him in the sedan.

The driver was facing the crowd again, trying to convince the people that Dave was attempting to hold him up for some money.

"He's faking!" he said, shouting between his dead lips. "These bums think they can get money by jumping in front of an automobile and then yelping that they're hurt. It's a good lesson for them; maybe they'll stop it now. I'm wise to them; I know when they're faking."

Dave opened his eyes and looked at me.

"Wait a minute, Mike," he said. "Put me down. I want to tell you something."

I laid him on the sidewalk as carefully as I could. He lay there looking up at me, his hand gripping my wrist.

"I just want to make sure you know where the half is, Mike," he said. "The half is in my right-hand pants pocket."

I was about to tell him again that it was all right about the fifty cents, and to forget it, when suddenly his grip on my wrist loosened and his eyes clouded.

During all the time I knelt there holding him in my arms I was trying to think of something to say to Dave before it was too late.

Before I could think of anything to tell him, the driver of the sedan elbowed closer and looked down at us.

"He's faking," he said. "The dirty bum's faking."

He elbowed his way out of the crowd and went toward his sedan. When he reached it, he shouted back over the heads of the people.

"There's nothing wrong with him! He can't put nothing over on me! I'm wise to these dirty bums. All they want is some money, and then they get well quick enough. The dirty bum's faking!"

"Sure, he's a bum," the fellow behind me said, his voice ringing as clear as a bell. "He might get some bum's blood on your goddam pretty upholstery."

Just then a policeman came running up, attracted by the crowd. He pushed the people away and poked me with his night-stick and asked what the trouble was. Before I could tell him, he struck me on the back with the billy.

"What the hell you guys blocking the street for?"

I told him Dave was dead.

He bent down and saw Dave for the first time.

"That's different," he said.

He turned around and walked half a block to a

call-box and rang up the city hospital for an ambulance. By the time he had come back, the man who was driving the sedan had left.

"Why didn't you take him to the hospital in the car that knocked him down?" the policeman asked, whirling his night-stick and looking down the street at a woman in front of a show window.

"Hell, can't you see he's a bum?" the fellow behind me said. "We didn't want to get bum's blood all over the goddam pretty upholstery."

The policeman stopped and looked at the fellow and me. He took a step forward.

"On your way, bums," he said, prodding us with his billy. "Clear out of here before I run you both in."

I ran back beside Dave and stood over him, a foot on each side of his body. The policeman jumped at me, swinging his billy and cursing.

All at once the street lights went black, and when I could see again, the fellow who had stayed with me was dragging me down the street towards the freight-yards. As we passed under the last street light, I looked up at him and saw the policeman's night-stick protruding from his coat pocket.

Masses of Men

Masses of Men

HUGH MILLER worked for the street-railway company. Hugh had a silver button, a gold button, a bronze watch-fob made like a trolley-car, and a small tin disk with the numeral 7 almost worn off. He had worked for the company for twenty-six years repairing tracks, and the company had once told him that some day he would be retired with a comfortable pension.

After all those years, Hugh was still trying to get along in the world. He still hoped to be made superintendent of construction. For some reason, though, he had never got far. He was still repairing tracks, replacing switch-frogs, and jacking up the rails to put in new crossties.

Even though there were other men who were stepped ahead when the time came to fill up the ranks, Hugh kept his job as a laborer, repairing the tracks year after year, and hoped he would be made superintendent of construction before he got too old to work any longer.

"I'll get it yet," he told himself. "I'll get it as sure as shooting. They've got to promote me some day, and I've been working long enough now to get it. I'll get it as sure as shooting."

Hugh had put off marrying Cora until he was promoted. Cora told him that she did not mind waiting a little longer, because she was working herself then in a store in town and earning as much as Hugh himself was. But after the twelfth year, Hugh decided that if he ever was going to get married, he ought to do it without further delay. He was growing old and though Cora was still as youthful in appearance as she was when they became engaged, she was beginning to complain of the long hours she had to stand on her feet behind the counter in the variety store.

"We'll get married right now," Hugh told her one Saturday night while they were riding home from downtown on his company pass. "There's no sense in waiting any longer. If you are ready, we'll be married next week. I've been thinking about it a long time, and there's no sense in waiting till I get promoted."

"I'd love to, Hugh," she said, clutching his arm in the crowded car. "I think it's silly to put it off any longer. I've been hoping for it to happen for I don't know how long. We don't have to wait until you get promoted. It would be all the nicer to have the promotion come while we are married."

They got off the car at the boulevard stop and

walked home slowly. They lived next door to each other, in boarding houses, and there was no hurry since it was Saturday night.

That was the beginning. They walked slowly down the dark street talking about next week, and Hugh kept saying to himself under his breath that he would surely get promoted the next time the company filled up the ranks. He was certain of it. He told Cora he was. She believed him.

After they were married, Hugh rented a five-room house not far from the car-barn. It was just a step down the alley from the tree-lined street where the trolleys passed all day and most of the night. It was a good house, for the money, and it was comfortable. Having their doorstep in an alley did not really matter much after all. They did not mind that. The house was almost on the corner, and the upstairs windows looked out over the tree-lined street. They could step out the front door, walk a few steps, and be in the street. It was not a bad place to live, and Cora liked it.

First there was a girl; they named her Pearl. Later there was a boy, John; after another year there was another girl, and they named her Ruby.

Hugh still looked forward to the time when he would be made superintendent of construction for the street-railway company, but after Ruby was born, he did not think about it any more. He somehow got out of the habit of thinking about it. Cora had stopped working in the variety store downtown; she stayed at home and attended to the house and cared for the children. She was beginning to wonder what she could do to her skin to keep it from turning so dark; in the meantime she hid her face when people came to the door for some reason or other. She knew there was nothing wrong with her skin; it was merely becoming darker and darker every day. But she wished she knew what to do about it. Her hair already had a wide streak of gray in it.

She never mentioned it to Hugh, but Hugh never talked any more, anyway. When he came home from work, he ate his supper and went to bed. She did not have a chance to tell Hugh anything like that. He was too tired to listen to her.

When Pearl, the oldest girl, was nine, Hugh was knocked down by an automobile one day, while he was jacking up a rail to replace a rotten crosstie, and run over and killed. The company sent his body home that evening, when the rest of the workers got off at five o'clock, and Cora did not know what to do. After she had put the children to bed, she went out and walked down the street until she met a policeman. She told him what had happened to Hugh, and he said he would have the body taken away early the next morning. She went back home and looked at

Hugh, but she could not notice any difference in him; at home, Hugh was always asleep.

Cora knew there would be a little money coming in from the company. She was certain there would be something, but she was afraid it would not be enough for them to live on until she could find work of some kind. When she thought about it more, she was afraid there would not even be enough to pay for Hugh's funeral and burial.

The policeman had the body taken away the next morning, and it was buried somewhere. Cora did not know where, but she did know there was nothing else to do about it. The children had to have food, and they had to have a little heat in the house.

She waited a month for the money to come from the street-railway company, and it still did not come. After that she went to the office and asked for it. There was no one there who seemed to know anything about the matter. Nobody in the big brick building had ever heard of Hugh Miller, and when they looked up the name in their records, no one was certain which Hugh Miller she was inquiring about. Cora stayed there all day, but when the people in the building went home at dark, she did not know what else to do except to go home, too.

After that she did not bother the people at the street-railway company any more. She did not have time to go there, for one thing, and she had a lot to do at home. The three children had to be taken care of, and she had to go out every day and find enough food to keep them from being hungry. Sometimes it took her all day long to get enough to feed them for just one small meal; other times she could find nothing at all for them to eat, but she kept on walking because the children had to be fed.

Pearl was going on ten. She was the oldest, and Ruby was still just a baby. But Pearl was growing up. She had long yellow hair and a blue gingham dress, and she tried to help her mother all she could. She cared for the other children while Cora was out trying to get some food, and at night she helped her mother put them to bed. After they were asleep, Cora would tell her about her father, Hugh.

"Your father worked for the street-railway company," she told Pearl. "The company would help us out, but they are so busy up there they can't seem to find time to do anything about it now. They would help us if they could get all the Hugh Millers who have worked for them straight in their minds. Your father was just one of them, and it's hard for the company to tell them apart."

"I can work," Pearl told her mother. "I'm old enough now. I'll see if I can find something to do. You take me with you, Mamma, and I'll ask about it.

John and Ruby can take care of each other if we lock them in a room before we go out."

"You're not very big for your age," Cora said. "People wouldn't believe you when you told them you were going on ten."

"But I can work. I'll show them how much I can do."

"Hugh worked for the street-railway company, Pearl. He was your father. Some day the company will help us out. They're busy right now. I don't like to bother them so much when they act like they are so busy."

Pearl went to bed telling her mother that she was old enough to work. Cora did not say anything else to her, but she could not think of any kind of work that Pearl was capable of doing.

The next morning John and Ruby went out early to bring back some wood for the stove. They had no shoes to wear, and their coats were not warm enough. It was mid-winter, but the ground was bare of snow. When they came back that afternoon, their feet were bleeding around the toes and their heels had cracked open in several places.

"Where's the firewood, John?" Cora asked him.

"We couldn't find any."

Cora put on her cloak, pulling it up around her head and shoulders, and went out into the alley. There was no wood of any kind there, but up at the other end there was a coal bin that sometimes overflowed into the narrow way. She filled her apron with coal and ran back to the house. The children huddled around the stove, shivering and whimpering, while she kindled the fire.

"I'm hungry, Mamma," Ruby said.

"I'll get you something to eat," Cora promised her.

"When are we going to have something to eat again?" John asked her.

"I'll bring you something when I come back."

Cora put on her cloak and went out into the alley. She ran to the street and stood there indecisively for several moments until she could make up her mind which direction she would take. She turned down the street this time, instead of going up it.

After she had run and walked for five or six blocks, she came to a cluster of one-storey suburban stores. There were several men standing at the curb in front of the buildings. They were waiting for a street car to take them downtown. The men turned and looked at Cora when they saw that she was running towards them.

"Mister, give me half a dollar for my children," she pleaded.

The men turned all the way around and looked her up and down. One of them laughed at her.

"Sister," one of them said, "I wouldn't give a dime for you and a dozen more like you."

The others laughed at what he had said. The trolley was coming down the street, its bell clanging. The men stepped out into the street and stood beside the tracks waiting for it to stop and take them aboard. Cora followed them into the middle of the street.

"Mister," she said to the man who had spoken to her, "Mister, what would you——"

"Don't call me 'Mister,' " he said angrily. "I don't like it. My name's Johnson."

The others laughed at her again. Johnson stepped forward and looked down at her while his friends continued laughing at her.

"Mr. Johnson," Cora said, "what would you give me half a dollar for?"

"What would I give you half a dollar for?" he asked.

"Yes, Mr. Johnson. What would you give it to me for?"

He turned around and winked at the other men before answering her. They urged him on.

"Have you got a girl at home?" he asked her.

"Yes, sir. I've got Pearl, and Ruby, too."

"Well, I couldn't give you half a dollar, but I might be able to give you a quarter."

The street car stopped and the door sprang open.

The motorman had a tin disk pinned to his coat that looked just like the one Hugh had.

The other two men hopped on, calling to Johnson to hurry. He looked at Cora for a moment longer, his hand on the street car, but when she continued to stand there with her mouth open, unable to say anything, he turned and jumped aboard.

Cora was left standing beside the tracks. When the car started, she stood on her toes and tried to see the man inside who had spoken to her. She called to him frantically, trying to make him understand her, and she waved her arms excitedly, attempting to attract his attention. All three of them ran to the rear end of the car and pressed their faces against the glass to see her better. Cora ran down the middle of the street, between the street-car rails, calling to them and trying to stop them, but the car was soon out of sight and she was left standing in the car tracks. She went to the sidewalk and walked back up the street until she had reached the corner in front of the stores where the men had been standing when she first saw them. When she got to the corner, she sat down on the curb to wait.

Cora did not know how long she had waited, but she had promised the children she would bring back some food when she returned, and she had to wait no matter how long the time was. But Johnson finally came back. He got off the street car and walked towards her at the curb. He was surprised to see her there, and he stopped before her and looked down at her in amazement. Cora was glad the other men had not come back with him.

She led him up the street, running ahead and urging him to hurry. Even though he followed her without protest, he did not walk fast enough to please Cora, and she was continually asking him to hurry. He stopped once and struck a match for his cigarette against an iron street-light pole, and Cora ran back and pulled at his coat, begging him to follow her as fast as he could.

When they got to the house, Cora awakened Pearl. The man stood close to the door, debating with himself whether to remain and see what happened or whether to leave before something did happen. Cora got behind him and held the door shut so he could not leave.

"How old is she?" he asked Cora.

"She's almost ten now."

"It's cold as hell in this house. Why don't you have some heat in here? You've got a stove there."

"Give me a quarter, and I'll try to get some coal somewhere," Cora said.

"Tell her to stand up."

"Stand up, Pearl," Cora told her.

Pearl shrank against the foot of the bed; she was bewildered and frightened. She wished to run to her mother, but the strange man was between them. She was afraid he would catch her before she could reach the door where Cora stood.

"You're lying to me," Johnson said. "She's nowhere near ten."

"I swear to God, Mr. Johnson, she's almost ten," Cora said. "Please, Mr. Johnson, don't go off now."

"Christ, how do I know this's not a shake-down?" he said, shivering and shaking.

"I swear before God, Mr. Johnson!"

Johnson looked around the room and saw John and Ruby asleep under the quilts on the bed.

"How old is the other girl?"

"She's going on eight."

"Christ!" he said.

"What's the matter, Mr. Johnson?"

"I don't believe you. You're lying to me. Neither one of them is over seven or eight."

"Pearl's almost ten, Mr. Johnson. I swear before God, she is. Please give me the quarter."

He walked across the room towards Pearl. She tried to run away, but Cora caught her and made her stand still beside the foot of the bed. Cora waited behind Johnson.

"Tell her to turn around," he said.

"Turn around, Pearl," Cora told her.

"Christ!" Johnson said, rubbing his face and neck with both hands.

"What's the matter?" Cora asked him.

"It's too damn cold in here," he said, his hands trembling. "My feet are frozen already. Why don't you build a fire in the stove?"

"If you'll give me the quarter, I'll try to get a little coal somewhere."

"How do I know you're on the level?" he asked her. "How do I know this is not a shake-down? I'm afraid of you. You don't look right to me. How do I know you won't go yelling for a cop the first thing?"

"I wouldn't do that. Give me the quarter."

"I'd be in a pretty fix, caught like that. They'd give me twenty years at hard labor. I'd never get out alive."

"I won't tell anybody, Mr. Johnson. I swear before God, I won't. Just give me the quarter."

Johnson pushed his hands into his pockets and looked at Pearl again. His hands were cold; his feet were, too. His breath looked like smoke in the cold house.

"Tell her to let me see her," he said.

"Let him see you, Pearl," Cora said.

Johnson waited, looking at her and at Cora. He

could not stand there freezing to death while waiting for Cora to make her obey.

"Hurry up, Pearl, and let him see you," Cora urged.

Pearl began to cry.

"They'd give me life for that," Johnson said, backing towards the door. "You'd get a cop after me before I could get out of the house. I don't like the way you look. Why don't you have some heat in here? You've got a stove."

"Honest to God, Mr. Johnson, I wouldn't tell on you," Cora pleaded. "Give me the quarter, and you can trust me."

"Get some heat in here first," he said. "My feet are freezing solid."

"I can't get any coal until you give me the quarter."

"You can go steal some, can't you?"

"Give me the quarter first, Mr. Johnson."

"How do I know you're on the level? I don't like the way you look. How do I know this's not a shakedown?"

"I swear to God, I won't tell on you, Mr. Johnson."

Johnson lit a cigarette and inhaled the smoke in the manner of a man gasping for breath. With his lungs and mouth and nostrils dense with smoke, he dropped the cigarette into the stove and thrust both hands back into his pants pockets.

"Tell her to come over here," he said.

"Go over there, Pearl."

Johnson bent down and looked at Pearl in the dim light. He straightened up once for a moment, and bent down again and looked at her more closely.

"They'd hang me before tomorrow night if they caught me," he said unevenly.

"Give me the quarter, Mr. Johnson, and I swear before God I won't tell anybody."

"Tell her to stand still."

"Stand still, Pearl."

"For God's sake get some heat in here."

"Give me the quarter first, Mr. Johnson," Cora begged.

"And then go out and tell a cop?" he said shrilly.

"Just give me the quarter first."

"You're crazy," he shouted at her. "I don't like the looks of you. How do I know what you'll do? You might run out of here the first thing yelling for a cop."

"Give me the quarter, and I'll get a little coal."

"And tell a cop."

"I swear I won't do that, Mr. Johnson. Give me the quarter, and I'll get some coal."

Johnson turned his back on Cora and went closer to Pearl. He took his hands out of his pants pockets and blew into them.

"Tell her to stop that crying."

"Stop crying, Pearl."

Johnson reached down and put his hands under Pearl's thick yellow hair, but the moment he touched her, she whirled around and ran to Cora.

"They'd screw my head off my neck so quick I wouldn't have a chance to think about it."

"Give me the quarter, Mr. Johnson, and I swear to God I won't tell on you."

He hesitated a moment; looking at Pearl, he shoved his hand into his pants pocket and brought out a twenty-five-cent piece. Cora grabbed it from his hand and bolted for the door.

"Wait a minute!" he shouted, running and catching her. "Come back here and tell her to keep still before you go."

"Keep still, Pearl," her mother told her.

"Hurry up and get some coal before I freeze to death in this place. And if you tell a policeman, I'll kill the last one of you before they take me. I ought to have better sense than to let you go out of here before I do. I don't like the way you look."

Cora ran to the door and into the alley before he could say anything more to her. She slammed the door and ran with all her might to the end of the alley. Without losing a moment, she raced down the street towards the one-storey stores.

After she had gone a block, she stopped and carefully placed the quarter on her tongue and closed her lips tightly so she would be sure not to drop it or lose it on the dark street.

One of the grocery stores was still open. She took the coin out of her mouth, pointing at the bread and pressed meat, and placed the money in the clerk's hand. He dropped the wet silver piece as though it were white-hot steel and wiped his hands on his apron.

"What's this?" he said. "What did you do to it?"

"Nothing," Cora said. "Hurry up!"

When Cora got back, the children were asleep. John and Ruby were rolled tightly in the quilts, and Pearl was lying on the bed with her coat over her. Her gingham dress was lying on the floor, marked with brown streaks of footprints. She had been crying, and the tears had not fully dried on her cheeks; her eyes were inflamed, and her face was swollen across the bridge of her nose.

Cora went to the side of the bed and threw the coat from her and looked down at her. Pearl had doubled herself into a knot, with her arms locked around her knees, and her head was thrust forward over her chest. Cora looked at her for a while, and then she carefully replaced the coat over her.

After unwrapping the bread and pressed meat, she stuffed the paper into the stove and struck a match to it. She drew her chair closer and bent forward so she could stretch her arms around the sides of the stove and feel the heat as much as possible before the wrapping paper burned out.

When the stove became cold again, Cora laid the bread and pressed meat on a chair beside her and rolled up in her quilt to wait for day to come. When the children woke up, they would find the food there for them.

Kneel to the Rising Sun

Kneel to the Rising Sun

A SHIVER went through Lonnie. He drew his hand away from his sharp chin, remembering what Clem had said. It made him feel now as if he were committing a crime by standing in Arch Gunnard's presence and allowing his face to be seen.

He and Clem had been walking up the road together that afternoon on their way to the filling station when he told Clem how much he needed rations. Clem stopped a moment to kick a rock out of the road, and said that if you worked for Arch Gunnard long enough, your face would be sharp enough to split the boards for your own coffin.

As Lonnie turned away to sit down on an empty box beside the gasoline pump, he could not help wishing that he could be as unafraid of Arch Gunnard as Clem was. Even if Clem was a Negro, he never hesitated to ask for rations when he needed something to eat; and when he and his family did not get enough, Clem came right out and told Arch so. Arch stood for that, but he swore that he was going to run Clem out of the country the first chance he got.

Lonnie knew without turning around that Clem

was standing at the corner of the filling station with two or three other Negroes and looking at him, but for some reason he was unable to meet Clem's eyes.

Arch Gunnard was siting in the sun, honing his jack-knife blade on his boot top. He glanced once or twice at Lonnie's hound, Nancy, who was lying in the middle of the road waiting for Lonnie to go home.

"That your dog, Lonnie?"

Jumping with fear, Lonnie's hand went to his chin to hide the lean face that would accuse Arch of short-rationing.

Arch snapped his fingers and the hound stood up, wagging her tail. She waited to be called.

"Mr. Arch, I—"

Arch called the dog. She began crawling towards them on her belly, wagging her tail a little faster each time Arch's fingers snapped. When she was several feet away, she turned over on her back and lay on the ground with her four paws in the air.

Dudley Smith and Jim Weaver, who were lounging around the filling station, laughed. They had been leaning against the side of the building, but they straightened up to see what Arch was up to.

Arch spat some more tobacco juice on his boot top and whetted the jack-knife blade some more.

"What kind of a hound dog is that, anyway, Lonnie?" Arch said. "Looks like to me it might be a ketch hound."

Lonnie could feel Clem Henry's eyes boring into the back of his head. He wondered what Clem would do if it had been his dog Arch Gunnard was snapping his fingers at and calling like that.

"His tail's way too long for a coon hound or a bird dog, ain't it, Arch?" somebody behind Lonnie said, laughing out loud.

Everybody laughed then, including Arch. They looked at Lonnie, waiting to hear what he was going to say to Arch.

"Is he a ketch hound, Lonnie?" Arch said, snapping his finger again.

"Mr. Arch, I—"

"Don't be ashamed of him, Lonnie, if he don't show signs of turning out to be a bird dog or a fox hound. Everybody needs a hound around the house that can go out and catch pigs and rabbits when you are in a hurry for them. A ketch hound is a mighty respectable animal. I've known the time when I was mighty proud to own one."

Everybody laughed.

Arch Gunnard was getting ready to grab Nancy by the tail. Lonnie sat up, twisting his neck until he caught a glimpse of Clem Henry at the other corner of the filling station. Clem was staring at him with unmistakable meaning, with the same look in his eyes he had had that afternoon when he said that nobody who worked for Arch Gunnard ought to stand for short-rationing. Lonnie lowered his eyes. He could not figure out how a Negro could be braver than he was. There were a lot of times like that when he would have given anything he had to be able to jump into Clem's shoes and change places with him.

"The trouble with this hound of yours, Lonnie, is that he's too heavy on his feet. Don't you reckon it would be a pretty slick little trick to lighten the load some, being as how he's a ketch hound to begin with?"

Lonnie remembered then what Clem Henry had said he would do if Arch Gunnard ever tried to cut off his dog's tail. Lonnie knew, and Clem knew, and everybody else knew, that that would give Arch the chance he was waiting for. All Arch asked, he had said, was for Clem Henry to overstep his place just one little half-inch, or to talk back to him with just one little short word, and he would do the rest. Everybody knew what Arch meant by that, especially if Clem did not turn and run. And Clem had not been known to run from anybody, after fifteen years in the country.

Arch reached down and grabbed Nancy's tail while Lonnie was wondering about Clem. Nancy acted as if she thought Arch were playing some kind of a game with her. She turned her head around until she could reach Arch's hand to lick it. He cracked her on the bridge of the nose with the end of the jack-knife.

"He's a mighty playful dog, Lonnie," Arch said, catching up a shorter grip on the tail, "but his wag-pole is way too long for a dog his size, especially when he wants to be a ketch hound."

Lonnie swallowed hard.

"Mr. Arch, she's a mighty fine rabbit tracker. I——"

"Shucks, Lonnie," Arch said, whetting the knife blade on the dog's tail, "I aint never seen a hound in all my life that needed a tail that long to hunt rabbits with. It's way too long for just a common, ordinary, everyday ketch hound."

Lonnie looked up hopefully at Dudley Smith and the others. None of them offered any help. It was useless for him to try to stop Arch, because Arch Gunnard would let nothing stand in his way when once he had set his head on what he wished to do. Lonnie knew that if he should let himself show any anger or resentment, Arch would drive him off the farm before sundown that night. Clem Henry was the only person there who would help him, but Clem . . .

The white men and the Negroes at both corners of the filling station waited to see what Lonnie was going to do about it. All of them hoped he would put up a fight for his hound. If anyone ever had the nerve to stop Arch Gunnard from cutting off a dog's tail, it might put an end to it. It was plain, though, that Lonnie, who was one of Arch's share-croppers, was afraid to speak up. Clem Henry might; Clem was the only one who might try to stop Arch, even if it meant trouble. And all of them knew that Arch would insist on running Clem out of the country, or filling him full of lead.

"I reckon it's all right with you, aint it, Lonnie?" Arch said. "I don't seem to hear no objections."

Clem Henry stepped forward several paces, and stopped.

Arch laughed, watching Lonnie's face, and jerked Nancy to her feet. The hound cried out in pain and surprise, but Arch made her be quiet by kicking her in the belly.

Lonnie winced. He could hardly bear to see anybody kick his dog like that.

"Mr. Arch, I . . ."

A contraction in his throat almost choked him for several moments, and he had to open his mouth wide and fight for breath. The other white men around him were silent. Nobody liked to see a dog kicked in the belly like that.

Lonnie could see the other end of the filling station

from the corner of his eye. He saw a couple of Negroes go up behind Clem and grasp his overalls. Clem spat on the ground, between outspread feet, but he did not try to break away from them.

"Being as how I don't hear no objections, I reckon it's all right to go ahead and cut it off," Arch said, spitting.

Lonnie's head went forward and all he could see of Nancy was her hind feet. He had come to ask for a slab of sowbelly and some molasses, or something. Now he did not know if he could ever bring himself to ask for rations, no matter how much hungrier they became at home.

"I always make it a habit of asking a man first," Arch said. "I wouldn't want to go ahead and cut off a tail if a man had any objections. That wouldn't be right. No, sir, it just wouldn't be fair and square."

Arch caught a shorter grip on the hound's tail and placed the knife blade on it two or three inches from the rump. It looked to those who were watching as if his mouth were watering, because tobacco juice began to trickle down the corners of his lips. He brought up the back of his hand and wiped his mouth.

A noisy automobile came plowing down the road through the deep red dust. Everyone looked up as it passed in order to see who was in it.

Lonnie glanced at it, but he could not keep his eyes

raised. His head fell downward once more until he could feel his sharp chin cutting into his chest. He wondered then if Arch had noticed how lean his face was.

"I keep two or three ketch hounds around my place," Arch said, honing the blade on the tail of the dog as if it were a razor strop until his actions brought smiles to the faces of the men grouped around him, "but I never could see the sense of a ketch hound having a long tail. It only gets in their way when I send them out to catch a pig or a rabbit for my supper."

Pulling with his left hand and pushing with his right, Arch Gunnard docked the hound's tail as quickly and as easily as if he were cutting a willow switch in the pasture to drive the cows home with. The dog sprang forward with the release of her tail until she was far beyond Arch's reach, and began howling so loud she could be heard half a mile away. Nancy stopped once and looked back at Arch, and then she sprang to the middle of the road and began leaping and twisting in circles. All that time she was yelping and biting at the bleeding stub of her tail.

Arch leaned backward and twirled the severed tail in one hand while he wiped the jack-knife blade on his boot sole. He watched Lonnie's dog chasing herself around in circles in the red dust.

Nobody had anything to say then. Lonnie tried not to watch his dog's agony, and he forced himself to keep from looking at Clem Henry. Then, with his eyes shut, he wondered why he had remained on Arch Gunnard's plantation all those past years, share-cropping for a mere living on short-rations, and becoming leaner and leaner all the time. He knew then how true it was what Clem had said about Arch's share-croppers' faces becoming sharp enough to hew their own coffins. His hands went to his chin before he knew what he was doing. His hand dropped when he had felt the bones of jaw and the exposed tendons of his cheeks.

As hungry as he was, he knew that even if Arch did give him some rations then, there would not be nearly enough for them to eat for the following week. Hatty, his wife, was already broken down from hunger and work in the fields, and his father, Mark Newsome, stone-deaf for the past twenty years, was always asking him why there was never enough food in the house for them to have a solid meal. Lonnie's head fell forward a little more, and he could feel his eyes becoming damp.

The pressure of his sharp chin against his chest made him so uncomfortable that he had to raise his head at last in order to ease the pain of it.

The first thing he saw when he looked up was Arch Gunnard twirling Nancy's tail in his left hand. Arch Gunnard had a trunk full of dogs' tails at home. He had been cutting off tails ever since anyone could remember, and during all those years he had accumulated a collection of which he was so proud that he kept the trunk locked and the key tied around his neck on a string. On Sunday afternoons when the preacher came to visit, or when a crowd was there to loll on the front porch and swap stories, Arch showed them off, naming each tail from memory just as well as if he had had a tag on it.

Clem Henry had left the filling station and was walking alone down the road towards the plantation. Clem Henry's house was in a cluster of Negro cabins below Arch's big house, and he had to pass Lonnie's house to get there. Lonnie was on the verge of getting up and leaving when he saw Arch looking at him. He did not know whether Arch was looking at his lean face, or whether he was watching to see if he were going to get up and go down the road with Clem.

The thought of leaving reminded him of his reason for being there. He had to have some rations before suppertime that night, no matter how short they were.

"Mr. Arch, I . . ."

Arch stared at him for a moment, appearing as if he had turned to listen to some strange sound unheard of before that moment.

Lonnie bit his lips, wondering if Arch was going to say anything about how lean and hungry he looked. But Arch was thinking about something else. He slapped his hand on his leg and laughed out loud.

"I sometimes wish niggers had tails," Arch said, coiling Nancy's tail into a ball and putting it into his pocket. "I'd a heap rather cut off nigger tails than dog tails. There'd be more to cut, for one thing."

Dudley Smith and somebody else behind them laughed for a brief moment. The laughter died out almost as suddenly as it had risen.

The Negroes who had heard Arch shuffled their feet in the dust and moved backwards. It was only a few minutes until not one was left at the filling station. They went up the road behind the red wooden building until they were out of sight.

Arch got up and stretched. The sun was getting low, and it was no longer comfortable in the October air. "Well, I reckon I'll be getting on home to get me some supper," he said.

He walked slowly to the middle of the road and stopped to look at Nancy retreating along the ditch.

"Nobody going my way?" he asked. "What's

wrong with you, Lonnie? Going home to supper, aint you?"

"Mr. Arch, I . . ."

Lonnie found himself jumping to his feet. His first thought was to ask for the sowbelly and molasses, and maybe some corn meal; but when he opened his mouth, the words refused to come out. He took several steps forward and shook his head. He did not know what Arch might say or do if he said "no."

"Hatty'll be looking for you," Arch said, turning his back and walking off.

He reached into his hip pocket and took out Nancy's tail. He began twirling it as he walked down the road towards the big house in the distance.

Dudley Smith went inside the filling station, and the others walked away.

After Arch had gone several hundred yards, Lonnie sat down heavily on the box beside the gas pump from which he had got up when Arch spoke to him. He sat down heavily, his shoulders drooping, his arms falling between his outspread legs.

Lonnie did not know how long his eyes had been closed, but when he opened them, he saw Nancy lying between his feet, licking the docked tail. While he watched her, he felt the sharp point of his chin cutting into his chest again. Presently the door behind him was slammed shut, and a minute later he could hear Dudley Smith walking away from the filling station on his way home.

II

Lonnie had been sleeping fitfully for several hours when he suddenly found himself wide awake. Hatty shook him again. He raised himself on his elbow and tried to see into the darkness of the room. Without knowing what time it was, he was able to determine that it was still nearly two hours until sunrise.

"Lonnie," Hatty said again, trembling in the cold night air, "Lonnie, your pa aint in the house."

Lonnie sat upright in bed.

"How do you know he aint?" he said.

"I've been lying here wide awake ever since I got in bed, and I heard him when he went out. He's been gone all that time."

"Maybe he just stepped out for a while," Lonnie said, turning and trying to see through the bedroom window.

"I know what I'm saying, Lonnie," Hatty insisted. "Your pa's been gone a heap too long."

Both of them sat without a sound for several minutes while they listened for Mark Newsome.

Lonnie got up and lit a lamp. He shivered while he was putting on his shirt, overalls, and shoes. He tied his shoelaces in hard knots because he couldn't see in the faint light. Outside the window it was almost pitch-dark, and Lonnie could feel the damp October air blowing against his face.

"I'll go help look," Hatty said, throwing the covers off and starting to get up.

Lonnie went to the bed and drew the covers back over her and pushed her back into place.

"You try to get some sleep, Hatty," he said; "you can't stay awake the whole night. I'll go bring Pa back."

He left Hatty, blowing out the lamp, and stumbled through the dark hall, feeling his way to the front porch by touching the wall with his hands. When he got to the porch, he could still barely see any distance ahead, but his eyes were becoming more accustomed to the darkness. He waited a minute, listening.

Feeling his way down the steps into the yard, he walked around the corner of the house and stopped to listen again before calling his father.

"Oh, Pa!" he said loudly. "Oh, Pa!"

He stopped under the bedroom window when he realized what he had been doing.

"Now that's a fool thing for me to be out here doing," he said, scolding himself. "Pa couldn't hear it thunder."

He heard a rustling of the bed.

"He's been gone long enough to get clear to the

crossroads, or more," Hatty said, calling through the window.

"Now you lay down and try to get a little sleep, Hatty," Lonnie told her. "I'll bring him back in no time."

He could hear Nancy scratching fleas under the house, but he knew she was in no condition to help look for Mark. It would be several days before she recovered from the shock of losing her tail.

"He's been gone a long time," Hatty said, unable to keep still.

"That don't make no difference," Lonnie said. "I'll find him sooner or later. Now you go on to sleep like I told you, Hatty."

Lonnie walked towards the barn, listening for some sound. Over at the big house he could hear the hogs grunting and squealing, and he wished they would be quiet so he could hear other sounds. Arch Gunnard's dogs were howling occasionally, but they were not making any more noise than they usually did at night, and he was accustomed to their howling.

Lonnie went to the barn, looking inside and out. After walking around the barn, he went into the field as far as the cotton shed. He knew it was useless, but he could not keep from calling his father time after time.

"Oh, Pa!" he said, trying to penetrate the darkness.

He went further into the field.

"Now, what in the world could have become of Pa?" he said, stopping and wondering where to look next.

After he had gone back to the front yard, he began to feel uneasy for the first time. Mark had not acted any more strangely during the past week than he ordinarily did, but Lonnie knew he was upset over the way Arch Gunnard was giving out short-rations. Mark had even said that, at the rate they were being fed, all of them would starve to death inside another three months.

Lonnie left the yard and went down the road towards the Negro cabins. When he got to Clem's house, he turned in and walked up the path to the door. He knocked several times and waited. There was no answer, and he rapped louder.

"Who's that?" he heard Clem say from bed.

"It's me," Lonnie said. "I've got to see you a minute, Clem. I'm out in the front yard."

He sat down and waited for Clem to dress and come outside. While he waited, he strained his ears to catch any sound that might be in the air. Over the fields towards the big house he could hear the fattening hogs grunt and squeal.

Clem came out and shut the door. He stood on the doorsill a moment speaking to his wife in bed, telling her he would be back and not to worry.

"Who's that?" Clem said, coming down into the yard.

Lonnie got up and met Clem half-way.

"What's the trouble?" Clem asked then, buttoning up his overall jumper.

"Pa's not in his bed," Lonnie said, "and Hatty says he's been gone from the house most all night. I went out in the field, and all around the barn, but I couldn't find a trace of him anywhere."

Clem then finished buttoning his jumper and began rolling a cigarette. He walked slowly down the path to the road. It was still dark, and it would be at least an hour before dawn made it any lighter.

"Maybe he was too hungry to stay in the bed any longer," Clem said. "When I saw him yesterday, he said he was so shrunk up and weak he didn't know if he could last much longer. He looked like his skin and bones couldn't shrivel much more."

"I asked Arch last night after suppertime for some rations—just a little piece of sowbelly and some molasses. He said he'd get around to letting me have some the first thing this morning."

"Why don't you tell him to give you full rations

or none?" Clem said. "If you knew you wasn't going to get none at all, you could move away and find a better man to share-crop for, couldn't you?"

"I've been loyal to Arch Gunnard for a long time now," Lonnie said. "I'd hate to haul off and leave him like that."

Clem looked at Lonnie, but he did not say anything more just then. They turned up the road towards the driveway that led up to the big house. The fattening hogs were still grunting and squealing in the pen, and one of Arch's hounds came down a cotton row beside the driveway to smell their shoes.

"Them fattening hogs always get enough to eat," Clem said. "There's not a one of them that don't weigh seven hundred pounds right now, and they're getting bigger every day. Besides taking all that's thrown to them, they make a lot of meals off the chickens that get in there to peck around."

Lonnie listened to the grunting of the hogs as they walked up the driveway towards the big house.

"Reckon we'd better get Arch up to help look for Pa?" Lonnie said. "I'd hate to wake him up, but I'm scared Pa might stray off into the swamp and get lost for good. He couldn't hear it thunder, even. I never could find him back there in all that tangle if he got into it."

Clem said something under his breath and went on towards the barn and hog pen. He reached the pen before Lonnie got there.

"You'd better come here quick," Clem said, turning around to see where Lonnie was.

Lonnie ran to the hog pen. He stopped and climbed half-way up the wooden-and-wire sides of the fence. At first he could see nothing, but gradually he was able to see the moving mass of black fattening hogs on the other side of the pen. They were biting and snarling at each other like a pack of hungry hounds turned loose on a dead rabbit.

Lonnie scrambled to the top of the fence, but Clem caught him and pulled him back.

"Don't go in that hog pen that way," he said. "Them hogs will tear you to pieces, they're that wild. They're fighting over something."

Both of them ran around the corner of the pen and got to the side where the hogs were. Down under their feet on the ground Lonnie caught a glimpse of a dark mass splotched with white. He was able to see it for a moment only, because one of the hogs trampled over it.

Clem opened and closed his mouth several times before he was able to say anything at all. He clutched at Lonnie's arm, shaking him.

"That looks like it might be your pa," he said. "I

swear before goodness, Lonnie, it does look like it."

Lonnie still could not believe it. He climbed to the top of the fence and began kicking his feet at the hogs, trying to drive them away. They paid no attention to him.

While Lonnie was perched there, Clem had gone to the wagon shed, and he ran back with two singletrees he had somehow managed to find there in the dark. He handed one to Lonnie, poking it at him until Lonnie's attention was drawn from the hogs long enough to take it.

Clem leaped over the fence and began swinging the singletree at the hogs. Lonnie slid down beside him, yelling at them. One hog turned on Lonnie and snapped at him, and Clem struck it over the back of the neck with enough force to drive it off momentarily.

By then Lonnie was able to realize what had happened. He ran to the mass of hogs, kicking them with his heavy stiff shoes and striking them on their heads with the iron-tipped singletree. Once he felt a stinging sensation, and looked down to see one of the hogs biting the calf of his leg. He had just enough time to hit the hog and drive it way before his leg was torn. He knew most of his overall leg had been ripped away, because he could feel the night air on his bare wet calf.

Clem had gone ahead and had driven the hogs back. There was no other way to do anything. They were in a snarling circle around them, and both of them had to keep the singletrees swinging back and forth all the time to keep the hogs off. Finally Lonnie reached down and got a grip on Mark's leg. With Clem helping, Lonnie carried his father to the fence and lifted him over to the other side.

They were too much out of breath for a while to say anything, or to do anything else. The snarling, fattening hogs were at the fence, biting the wood and wire, and making more noise than ever.

While Lonnie was searching in his pockets for a match, Clem struck one. He held the flame close to Mark Newsome's head.

They both stared unbelievingly, and then Clem blew out the match. There was nothing said as they stared at each other in the darkness.

Clem walked several steps away, and turned and came back beside Lonnie.

"It's him, though," Clem said, sitting down on the ground. "It's him, all right."

"I reckon so," Lonnie said. He could think of nothing else to say then.

They sat on the ground, one on each side of Mark, looking at the body. There had been no sign of life in the body beside them since they had first touched it. The face, throat, and stomach had been completely devoured.

"You'd better go wake up Arch Gunnard," Clem said after a while.

"What for?" Lonnie said. "He can't help none now. It's too late for help."

"Makes no difference," Clem insisted. "You'd better go wake him up and let him see what there is to see. If you wait till morning, he might take it into his head to say the hogs didn't do it. Right now is the time to get him up so he can see what his hogs did."

Clem turned around and looked at the big house. The dark outline against the dark sky made him hesitate.

"A man who short-rations tenants ought to have to sit and look at that till it's buried."

Lonnie looked at Clem fearfully. He knew Clem was right, but he was scared to hear a Negro say anything like that about a white man.

"You oughtn't talk like that about Arch," Lonnie said. "He's in bed asleep. He didn't have a thing to do with it. He didn't have no more to do with it than I did."

Clem laughed a little, and threw the singletree on the ground between his feet. After letting it lie there a little while, he picked it up and began beating the ground with it.

Lonnie got to his feet slowly. He had never seen Clem act like that before, and he did not know what to think about it. He left without saying anything and walked stiffly to the house in the darkness to wake up Arch Gunnard.

III

Arch was hard to wake up. And even after he was awake, he was in no hurry to get up. Lonnie was standing outside the bedroom window, and Arch was lying in bed six or eight feet away. Lonnie could hear him toss and grumble.

"Who told you to come and wake me up in the middle of the night?" Arch said.

"Well, Clem Henry's out here, and he said maybe you'd like to know about it."

Arch tossed around on the bed, flailing the pillow with his fists.

"You tell Clem Henry I said that one of these days he's going to find himself turned inside out, like a coat-sleeve."

Lonnie waited doggedly. He knew Clem was right in insisting that Arch ought to wake up and come out there to see what had happened. Lonnie was afraid to go back to the barnyard and tell Clem that Arch was not coming. He did not know, but he had a feeling that Clem might go into the bedroom and drag Arch out of bed. He did not like to think of anything like that taking place.

"Are you still out there, Lonnie?" Arch shouted.

"I'm right here, Mr. Arch. I—"

"If I wasn't so sleepy, I'd come out there and take a stick and—I don't know what I wouldn't do!"

Lonnie met Arch at the back step. On the way out to the hog pen Arch did not speak to him. Arch walked heavily ahead, not even waiting to see if Lonnie was coming. The lantern that Arch was carrying cast long flat beams of yellow light over the ground; and when they got to where Clem was waiting beside Mark's body, the Negro's face shone in the night like a highly polished plowshare.

"What was Mark doing in my hog pen at night, anyway?" Arch said, shouting at them both.

Neither Clem nor Lonnie replied. Arch glared at them for not answering. But no matter how many times he looked at them, his eyes returned each time to stare at the torn body of Mark Newsome on the ground at his feet.

"There's nothing to be done now," Arch said finally. "We'll just have to wait till daylight and send for the undertaker." He walked a few steps away. "Looks like you could have waited till morning in the first place. There wasn't no sense in getting me up."

He turned his back and looked sideways at Clem. Clem stood up and looked him straight in the eyes.

"What do you want, Clem Henry?" he said. "Who told you to be coming around my house in the middle of the night? I don't want niggers coming here except when I send for them."

"I couldn't stand to see anybody eaten up by the hogs, and not do anything about it," Clem said.

"You mind your own business," Arch told him. "And when you talk to me, take off your hat, or you'll be sorry for it. It wouldn't take much to make me do you up the way you belong."

Lonnie backed away. There was a feeling of uneasiness around them. That was how trouble between Clem and Arch always began. He had seen it start that way dozens of times before. As long as Clem turned and went away, nothing happened, but sometimes he stayed right where he was and talked up to Arch just as if he had been a white man, too.

Lonnie hoped it would not happen this time. Arch was already mad enough about being waked up in the middle of the night, and Lonnie knew there was no limit to what Arch would do when he got good and mad at a Negro. Nobody had ever seen him kill a Negro, but he had said he had, and he told people that he was not scared to do it again.

"I reckon you know how he came to get eaten up

by the hogs like that," Clem said, looking straight at Arch.

Arch whirled around.

"Are you talking to me . . . ?"

"I asked you that," Clem stated.

"God damn you, yellow-blooded . . ." Arch yelled.

He swung the lantern at Clem's head. Clem dodged, but the bottom of it hit his shoulder, and it was smashed to pieces. The oil splattered on the ground, igniting in the air from the flaming wick. Clem was lucky not to have it splash on his face and overalls.

"Now, look here . . ." Clem said.

"You yellow-blooded nigger," Arch said, rushing at him. "I'll teach you to talk back to me. You've got too big for your place for the last time. I've been taking too much from you, but I aint doing it no more."

"Mr. Arch, I . . ." Lonnie said, stepping forward partly between them. No one heard him.

Arch stood back and watched the kerosene flicker out on the ground.

"You know good and well why he got eaten up by the fattening hogs," Clem said, standing his ground. "He was so hungry he had to get up out of bed in the middle of the night and come up here in the dark trying to find something to eat. Maybe he was trying to find the smokehouse. It makes no difference, either way. He's been on short-rations like everybody else working on your place, and he was so old he didn't know where else to look for food except in your smokehouse. You know good and well that's how he got lost u· here in the dark and fell in the hog pen."

The kerosene had died out completely. In the last faint flare, Arch had reached down and grabbed up the singletree that had been lying on the ground where Lonnie had dropped it.

Arch raised the singletree over his head and struck with all his might at Clem. Clem dodged, but Arch drew back again quickly and landed a blow on his arm just above the elbow before Clem could dodge it. Clem's arm dropped to his side, dangling lifelessly.

"You Goddamn yellow-blooded nigger!" Arch shouted. "Now's your time, you black bastard. I've been waiting for the chance to teach you your lesson. And this's going to be one you won't never forget."

Clem felt the ground with his feet until he had located the other singletree. He stooped down and got it. Raising it, he did not try to hit Arch, but held it in front of him so he could ward off Arch's blows at his head. He continued to stand his ground, not giving Arch an inch.

"Drop that singletree," Arch said.

"I won't stand here and let you beat me like that," Clem protested.

"By God, that's all I want to hear," Arch said, his mouth curling. "Nigger, your time has come, by God!"

He swung once more at Clem, but Clem turned and ran towards the barn. Arch went after him a few steps and stopped. He threw aside the singletree and turned and ran back to the house.

Lonnie went to the fence and tried to think what was best for him to do. He knew he could not take sides with a Negro, in the open, even if Clem had helped him, and especially after Clem had talked to Arch in the way he wished he could himself. He was a white man, and to save his life he could not stand to think of turning against Arch, no matter what happened.

Presently a light burst through one of the windows of the house, and he heard Arch shouting at his wife to take her up.

When he saw Arch's wife go to the telephone, Lonnie realized what was going to happen. She was calling up the neighbors and Arch's friends. They would not mind getting up in the night when they found out what was going to take place.

Out behind the barn he could hear Clem calling

him. Leaving the yard, Lonnie felt his way out there in the dark.

"What's the trouble, Clem?" he said.

"I reckon my time has come," Clem said. "Arch Gunnard talks that way when he's good and mad. He talked just like he did that time he carried Jim Moffin off to the swamp—and Jim never came back."

"Arch wouldn't do anything like that to you, Clem," Lonnie said excitedly, but he knew better.

Clem said nothing.

"Maybe you'd better strike out for the swamps till he changes his mind and cools off some," Lonnie said. "You might be right, Clem."

Lonnie could feel Clem's eyes burning into him.

"Wouldn't be no sense in that, if you'd help me," Clem said. "Wouldn't you stand by me?"

Lonnie trembled as the meaning of Clem's suggestion became clear to him. His back was to the side of the barn, and he leaned against it while sheets of black and white passed before his eyes.

"Wouldn't you stand by me?" Clem asked again.

"I don't know what Arch would say to that," Lonnie told him haltingly.

Clem walked away several paces. He stood with his back to Lonnie while he looked across the field towards the quarter where his home was.

"I could go in that little patch of woods out there

and stay still they get tired of looking for me," Clem said, turning around to see Lonnie.

"You'd better go somewhere," Lonnie said uneasily. "I know Arch Gunnard. He's hard to handle when he makes up his mind to do something he wants to do. I couldn't stop him an inch. Maybe you'd better get clear out of the country, Clem."

"I couldn't do that, and leave my family down there across the field," Clem said.

"He's going to get you if you don't."

"If you'd only sort of help me out a little, he wouldn't. I would only have to go and hide out in that little patch of woods over there a while. Looks like you could do that for me, being as how I helped you find your pa when he was in the hog pen."

Lonnie nodded, listening for sounds from the big house. He continued to nod at Clem while Clem was waiting to be assured.

"If you're going to stand up for me," Clem said, "I can just go over there in the woods and wait till they get it off their minds. You won't be telling them where I'm at, and you could say I struck out for the swamp. They wouldn't ever find me without bloodhounds."

"That's right," Lonnie said, listening for sounds of Arch's coming out of the house. He did not wish to be found back there behind the barn where Arch could accuse him of talking to Clem.

The moment Lonnie replied, Clem turned and ran off into the night. Lonnie went after him a few steps, as if he had suddenly changed his mind about helping him, but Clem was lost in the darkness by then.

Lonnie waited for a few minutes, listening to Clem crashing through the underbrush in the patch of woods a quarter of a mile away. When he could hear Clem no longer, he went around the barn to meet Arch.

Arch came out of the house carrying his double-barreled shotgun and the lantern he had picked up in the house. His pockets were bulging with shells.

"Where is that damn nigger, Lonnie?" Arch asked him. "Where'd he go to?"

Lonnie opened his mouth, but no words came out.

"You know which way he went, don't you?"

Lonnie again tried to say something, but there were no sounds. He jumped when he found himself nodding his head to Arch.

"Mr. Arch, I—"

"That's all right, then," Arch said. "That's all I need to know now. Dudley Smith and Tom Hawkins and Frank and Dave Howard and the rest will be here in a minute, and you can stay right here so you can show us where he's hiding out."

Frantically Lonnie tried to say something. Then he reached for Arch's sleeve to stop him, but Arch had gone.

Arch ran around the house to the front yard. Soon a car came racing down the road, its headlights lighting up the whole place, hog pen and all. Lonnie knew it was probably Dudley Smith, because his was the first house in that direction, only half a mile away. While he was turning into the driveway, several other automobiles came into sight, both up the road and down it.

Lonnie trembled. He was afraid Arch was going to tell him to point out where Clem had gone to hide. Then he knew Arch would tell him. He had promised Clem he would not do that. But try as he might, he could not make himself believe that Arch Gunnard would do anything more than whip Clem.

Clem had not done anything that called for lynching. He had not raped a white woman, he had not shot at a white man; he had only talked back to Arch, with his hat on. But Arch was mad enough to do anything; he was mad enough at Clem not to stop at anything short of lynching.

The whole crowd of men was swarming around him before he realized it. And there was Arch clutching his arm and shouting into his face.

"Mr. Arch, I . . ."

Lonnie recognized every man in the feeble dawn.

They were excited, and they looked like men on the last lap of an all-night foxhunting party. Their shotguns and pistols were held at their waist, ready for the kill.

"What's the matter with you, Lonnie?" Arch said, shouting into his ear. "Wake up and say where Clem Henry went to hide out. We're ready to go get him."

Lonnie remembered looking up and seeing Frank Howard dropping yellow twelve-gauge shells into the breech of his gun. Frank bent forward so he could hear Lonnie tell Arch where Clem was hiding.

"You aint going to kill Clem this time, are you, Mr. Arch?" Lonnie asked.

"Kill him?" Dudley Smith repeated. "What do you reckon I've been waiting all this time for if it wasn't for a chance to get Clem. That nigger has had it coming to him ever since he came to this county. He's a bad nigger, and it's coming to him."

"It wasn't exactly Clem's fault," Lonnie said. "If Pa hadn't come up here and fell in the hog pen, Clem wouldn't have had a thing to do with it. He was helping me, that's all."

"Shut up, Lonnie," somebody shouted at him. "You're so excited you don't know what you're saying. You're taking up for a nigger when you talk like that."

People were crowding around him so tightly he

felt as if he were being squeezed to death. He had to get some air, get his breath, get out of the crowd.

"That's right," Lonnie said.

He heard himself speak, but he did not know what he was saying.

"But Clem helped me find Pa when he got lost looking around for something to eat."

"Shut up, Lonnie," somebody said again. "You damn fool, shut up!"

Arch grabbed his shoulder and shook him until his teeth rattled. Then Lonnie realized what he had been saying.

"Now, look here, Lonnie," Arch shouted. "You must be out of your head, because you know good and well you wouldn't talk like a nigger-lover in your right mind."

"That's right," Lonnie said, trembling all over. "I sure wouldn't want to talk like that."

He could still feel the grip on his shoulder where Arch's strong fingers had hurt him.

"Did Clem go to the swamp, Lonnie?" Dudley Smith said. "Is that right, Lonnie?"

Lonnie tried to shake his head; he tried to nod his head. Then Arch's fingers squeezed his thin neck. Lonnie looked at the men wild-eyed.

"Where's Clem hiding, Lonnie?" Arch demanded, squeezing.

Lonnie went three or four steps towards the barn. When he stopped, the men behind him pushed forward again. He found himself being rushed behind the barn and beyond it.

"All right, Lonnie," Arch said. "Now which way?"

Lonnie pointed towards the patch of woods where the creek was. The swamp was in the other direction.

"He said he was going to hide out in that little patch of woods along the creek over there, Mr. Arch," Lonnie said. "I reckon he's over there now."

Lonnie felt himself being swept forward, and he stumbled over the rough ground trying to keep from being knocked down and trampled upon. Nobody was talking, and everyone seemed to be walking on tiptoes. The gray light of early dawn was increasing enough both to hide them and to show the way ahead.

Just before they reached the fringe of the woods, the men separated, and Lonnie found himself a part of the circle that was closing in on Clem.

Lonnie was alone, and there was nobody to stop him, but he was unable to move forward or backward. It began to be clear to him what he had done.

Clem was probably up a tree somewhere in the woods ahead, but by that time he had been surrounded on all sides. If he should attempt to break and run, he would be shot down like a rabbit.

Lonnie sat down on a log and tried to think what to do. The sun would be up in a few more minutes, and as soon as it came up, the men would close in on the creek and Clem. He would have no chance at all among all those shotguns and pistols.

Once or twice he saw the flare of a match through the underbrush where some of the men were lying in wait. A whiff of cigarette smoke struck his nostrils, and he found himself wondering if Clem could smell it wherever he was in the woods.

There was still no sound anywhere around him, and he knew that Arch Gunnard and the rest of the men were waiting for the sun, which would in a few minutes come up behind him in the east.

It was light enough by that time to see plainly the rough ground and the tangled underbrush and the curling bark on the pine trees.

The men had already begun to creep forward, guns raised as if stalking a deer. The woods were not large, and the circle of men would be able to cover it in a few minutes at the rate they were going forward. There was still a chance that Clem had slipped through the circle before dawn broke, but Lonnie felt that he was still there. He began to feel then that Clem was there because he himself had placed him there for the men to find more easily.

Lonnie found himself moving forward, drawn into the narrowing circle. Presently he could see the men all around him in dim outline. Their eyes were searching the heavy green pine tops as they went forward from tree to tree.

"Oh, Pa!" he said in a hoarse whisper. "Oh, Pa!"

He went forward a few steps, looking into the bushes and up into the tree tops. When he saw the other men again, he realized that it was not Mark Newsome being sought. He did not know what had made him forget like that.

The creeping forward began to work into the movement of Lonnie's body. He found himself springing forward on his toes, and his body was leaning in that direction. It was like creeping up on a rabbit when you did not have a gun to hunt with.

He forgot again what he was doing there. The springing motion in his legs seemed to be growing stronger with each step. He bent forward so far he could almost touch the ground with his fingertips. He could not stop now. He was keeping up with the circle of men.

The fifteen men were drawing closer and closer together. The dawn had broken enough to show the time on the face of a watch. The sun was beginning to color the sky above.

Lonnie was far in advance of anyone else by then. He could not hold himself back. The strength in his legs was more than he could hold in check.

He had for so long been unable to buy shells for his gun that he had forgotten how much he liked to hunt.

The sound of the men's steady creeping had become a rhythm in his ears.

"Here's the bastard!" somebody shouted, and there was a concerted crashing through the dry underbrush. Lonnie dashed forward, reaching the tree almost as quickly as anyone else.

He could see everybody with guns raised, and far into the sky above the sharply outlined face of Clem Henry gleamed in the rising sun. His body was hugging the slender top of the pine.

Lonnie did not know who was the first to fire, but the rest of the men did not hesitate. There was a deafening roar as the shotguns and revolvers flared and smoked around the trunk of the tree.

He closed his eyes; he was afraid to look again at the face above. The firing continued without break. Clem hugged the tree with all his might, and then, with the far-away sound of splintering wood, the top of the tree and Clem came crashing through the lower limbs to the ground. The body, sprawling and torn, landed on the ground with a thud that stopped Lonnie's heart for a moment.

He turned, clutching for the support of a tree, as the firing began once more. The crumpled body was tossed time after time, like a sackful of kittens being killed with an automatic shotgun, as charges of lead were fired into it from all sides. A cloud of dust rose from the ground and drifted overhead with the choking odor of burned powder.

Lonnie did not remember how long the shooting lasted. He found himself running from tree to tree, clutching at the rough pine bark, stumbling wildly towards the cleared ground. The sky had turned from gray to red when he emerged in the open, and as he ran, falling over the hard clods in the plowed field, he tried to keep his eyes on the house ahead.

Once he fell and found it almost impossible to rise again to his feet. He struggled to his knees, facing the round red sun. The warmth gave him the strength to rise to his feet, and he muttered unintelligibly to himself. He tried to say things he had never thought to say before.

When he got home, Hatty was waiting for him in the yard. She had heard the shots in the woods, and she had seen him stumbling over the hard clods in the field, and she had seen him kneeling there looking straight into the face of the sun. Hatty was trembling as she ran to Lonnie to find out what the matter was.

Once in his own yard, Lonnie turned and looked for a second over his shoulder. He saw the men climbing over the fence at Arch Gunnard's. Arch's wife was standing on the back porch, and she was speaking to them.

"Where's your pa, Lonnie?" Hatty said. "And what in the world was all that shooting in the woods for?" Lonnie stumbled forward until he had reached the front porch. He fell upon the steps.

"Lonnie, Lonnie!" Hattie was saying. "Wake up and tell me what in the world is the matter. I've never seen the like of all that's going on."

"Nothing," Lonnie said. "Nothing."

"Well, if there's nothing the matter, can't you go up to the big house and ask for a little piece of streak-of-lean? We aint got a thing to cook for breakfast. Your pa's going to be hungrier than ever after being up walking around all night."

"What?" Lonnie said, his voice rising to a shout as he jumped to his feet.

"Why, I only said go up to the big house and get a little piece of streak-of-lean, Lonnie. That's all I said."

He grabbed his wife about the shoulders.

"Meat?" he yelled, shaking her roughly.

"Yes," she said, pulling away from him in surprise. "Couldn't you go ask Arch Gunnard for a little bit of streak-of-lean?"

Lonnie slumped down again on the steps, his hands falling between his outspread legs and his chin falling on his chest.

"No," he said almost inaudibly. "No. I aint hungry."